A Shaky

"I can see the landing strip [...] Frank said. "Check the regula[...] you, Joe?"

"Roger," the younger Hardy replied. He flicked a switch on the control panel and a light came on. A moment later whirring electric motors extended the wheels below the airplane's pontoons. "Landing gear: check," Joe said.

The plane's engine sputtered.

"What's wrong?" Callie asked.

"I don't know," Frank replied. "We're losing power. Joe, help me out here."

The two brothers began methodically checking controls and throwing switches. Despite their efforts the engine's coughing grew steadily worse.

With a final gasp the engine stopped. The small plane plunged toward the sea.

The Hardy Boys
Mystery Stories

Available from ALADDIN Paperbacks

HARDY BOYS®

#180
Typhoon Island

FRANKLIN W. DIXON

Aladdin Paperbacks

New York London Toronto Sydney Singapore

This book is a work of fiction. Any references to historical events, real people, or real locales are used fictitiously. Other names, characters, places, and incidents are the product of the author's imagination, and any resemblance to actual events or locales or persons, living or dead, is entirely coincidental.

First Aladdin Paperbacks edition August 2003
Copyright © 2003 by Simon & Schuster, Inc.

ALADDIN PAPERBACKS
An imprint of Simon & Schuster
Children's Publishing Division
1230 Avenue of the Americas
New York, NY 10020

The text of this book was set in New Caledonia.

Printed in the United States of America
2 4 6 8 10 9 7 5 3 1

THE HARDY BOYS MYSTERY STORIES is a trademark of Simon & Schuster, Inc.

THE HARDY BOYS and colophon are registered trademarks of Simon & Schuster, Inc.

Library of Congress Control Number 2002115457

ISBN 0-689-85884-1

Contents

Typhoon Island

1 Plunge into Paradise

"Don't worry, Mom," Callie Shaw said into the phone. "I'm sure the weather will be fine." She covered the phone's receiver with her hand and mouthed, "I'll be off in a minute," to her friends standing nearby.

Frank Hardy arched his eyebrows at his girlfriend and pointed toward his watch.

Callie nodded, indicating that she knew they were running late for their flight.

Frank looked at his brother, Joe, and Joe's girlfriend, Iola Morton, and shrugged. Joe and Iola shrugged back.

Callie motioned for them to keep quiet. "Yes," she said into the phone, "I'll call when we get to San Esteban. Yes. I've gotta run. Yeah. Okay. Give my love to Dad. Bye." She hung up the phone and walked toward her friends and their luggage. "Sorry about that," she said. "If cell phones worked down here, I could have called on the way."

The four teens began to walk quickly down the street, heading toward where they were supposed to pick up their rental plane. "I don't remember whether cell phones work on San Esteban or not," Joe said.

"Having no phones might actually *add* to the island's 'get-away-from-it-all' feeling," Iola noted.

"I suppose," Callie said, "but here on Kendall Key it's just a pain."

"Any trouble at home?" Frank asked, putting his arm around his girlfriend's shoulder.

Callie tousled Frank's hair playfully. "Mom says she's concerned about a tropical storm heading this way," she replied. "Mostly, though, she's just got worried-parent syndrome. Even though the four of us have been planning this vacation for months, and even though Iola has family on San Esteban, my folks *still* aren't used to their little girl going off on her own."

Iola smiled. "My big brother cured my parents of that—at least a bit."

"Yeah," Joe added, "after wondering what trouble Chet was getting into all these years, your folks have it easy with you."

Iola laughed. The warm Kendall Key wind tugged

at her dark hair, and she pushed her bangs back out of her eyes. "I should point out, Joe, that most of the 'trouble' Chet has gotten into has involved you and Frank."

Both Hardys grinned. "We may be good at getting people into trouble . . . ," Joe began.

"But we're even better at getting them *out*," Frank finished.

"Well, no trouble on this vacation, please," Callie said. "I've worked too long and hard saving up money for this trip. The only thing I want to do on San Esteban is relax."

"Your wish is our command," Frank said, bowing dramatically.

The four friends walked quickly across the crowded downtown boulevard toward the dock. San Esteban, their destination, was only a short flight away from Kendall Key, which was just off the Florida coast.

San Esteban was not a very large island in the Caribbean, but it was an independent country with its own elected government. Several small cities dotted its coast. The interior of the country was filled with mountains and jungles. Most of the life of San Esteban centered on its shores, and tourism was its main industry. Its beaches were famous for their soft white sand, and its people well-known for their hospitality.

Though the capital of San Esteban had a large

airport, there were no direct flights to the coastal city of Nuevo Esteban, where the teens would be vacationing. Fortunately Frank and Joe had their pilot's licenses, and the group had saved enough money to charter a small plane for the trip to the island and back.

Joe checked his watch. "We'll be lucky if they haven't rented our plane out from under us," he said. "That late connection really cost us time."

"We've got the plane for half a day," Frank said, "so it shouldn't be a problem. I called them before we made the connecting flight to alert them we might be late."

"I'm more worried about meeting up with Iola's cousin," Callie said. "There's no way we're going to get to San Esteban by the time we were supposed to meet her."

"Don't sweat it," Iola replied. "I can call Angela at a pay phone where she works. She told me her job puts her close to the airport."

"Someone told me it wasn't very far to the rental office, either," Frank noted. "Though I'm starting to wish that we'd taken a cab from the airport."

"What I want to know," Callie said, "is why the airplane rental office isn't *at* the airport."

"Well," Joe replied, coming to a stop at the end of the street, "take a look."

Before them stretched a long, wide wooden dock lined with numerous smaller piers that jutted out into the ocean. Fishermen stood on the wharf repairing their gear and working on their boats. A few tourists darted among them, some sightseeing, others chartering fishing boats.

At the far end of the dock stood a small plywood shack with a big sign propped on top of the roof. Hand-painted red letters on the sign read RUIZ BOAT & PLANE RENTALS.

Joe looked at the weathered building and the fading sign, and frowned. "Not a storefront that inspires confidence."

Frank shrugged. "This isn't Bayport, Joe," he said. "Besides, the island's chamber of commerce recommended it."

"I'm thinking there may not have been a lot of choices," Callie said.

"Other rental offices go to the island," Iola replied, "but according to the travel agency, this is the only one that sends planes to Nuevo Esteban."

"Well," Joe said, "I guess it's either this or we cancel our vacation." He smiled wryly and adjusted his travel bag strap on his shoulder. "Come on."

They hauled their luggage up to the service window at the front of the shack. Despite its outward appearance, the inside of Ruiz Rentals looked fairly clean and well organized. A short, thin man wearing a white muscle shirt and an old Boston Red Sox cap sat behind the small table that served as a desk. His hair was dark and curly, and at least three days' growth of beard decorated his chin. He smiled, showing a missing tooth in front.

"Hello," he said, "may I help you?" He spoke with a slight Caribbean accent.

"We're Frank and Joe Hardy," Frank said. "We have a plane reserved."

"I wondered when you would get here," the man said. "I almost rented your plane out." He smiled. "This is not high season, but there's still quite a bit of demand."

"But we called from the airport," Joe said defensively.

"You must have spoken to my brother, Pablo, on San Esteban," the man said. He handed a small stack of forms to Joe. "Sometimes the phones between here and there do not work so well. I'm Jose Ruiz. Pablo runs the business, but I help him out on Kendall Key sometimes. Please read the rental agreement while I swipe your credit card. Then I'll show you the plane."

Frank handed Jose his card, and the Hardys read and signed the agreement. It included the usual insurance clauses and waiver of liability. Jose returned the credit card and gave Frank the slip; Frank signed it.

Jose opened a door in the side of the shack and joined the teens outside. He handed a set of airplane keys and copies of the rental agreement to the Hardys. "Take these," he said with a smile, "and follow me."

The rental agent and the four teens walked to the boardwalk's rail. Jose pointed over to an airplane that bobbed on the water next to a short, floating metal pier. The plane was an older single-prop model with pontoons on the bottom, and RUIZ RENTALS and a serial number were stenciled on the tail.

Frank frowned. "I thought we were getting a Sullivan Brothers amphibian, not a converted Stationair," Frank said.

"Sorry," Jose replied with a shrug. "The plane we planned to give you has some mechanical trouble."

"Isn't that a Sullivan amphibian sitting there, right next to the Stationair?" Joe asked. He pointed to a larger, newer plane that was rolling gently on the waves nearby.

"That's the one with the engine problem, hombre," Jose said. "Don't worry, I adjusted your price. See?" He took the copy of the rental receipt from Joe and pointed to the bottom line.

Joe and Frank glanced at the figure on the paper, then at each other, and finally at their girlfriends. Iola and Callie looked hopeful and clutched their travel bags. Clearly the brothers couldn't turn down the substitute plane at this point.

"Well," Frank said, "I guess it'll have to do."

Jose smiled. "Excellent. She's in fine shape.

Passed inspection just last week. I know you'll have fun flying her."

"Just as long as she gets us to San Esteban," Joe replied.

"I guarantee it," Jose said. "My brother would kill me otherwise! Do you need help with your bags?"

"We can manage," Iola said. She, Callie, and the brothers picked up their luggage and toted it down the wharf to the small metal dock. They crossed to the airplane, unlocked the door, and loaded in their belongings. Finally they climbed in themselves.

Frank seated himself behind the pilot's yoke while Joe took the copilot position. "We'll trade on the way back," Frank said.

"That's okay," Joe replied. "You've got more experience with this type of plane than I do."

"This isn't the *newest* plane, is it?" Callie said as she buckled herself in. She looked around the cabin, clearly a bit uneasy.

"Sometimes vacationers can't be choosers," Frank replied. "It's either this or wait on Kendall Key until they get the Sullivan plane fixed."

"I'm not waiting another minute to start my vacation," Iola said firmly. "Let's get this bird in the air. Next stop: paradise."

"Please leave your troubles at the dock before boarding," Joe added in an official-sounding voice.

He and Frank went over the preflight checklist, then started up the engine. The old plane sputtered a bit, causing the girls to shift in their seats. Soon, though, the brothers had the engine purring like a contented pussycat. Joe cast the plane off, and Frank pulled them away from the dock.

They taxied out past some fishing boats and into the area of the harbor designated for takeoffs and landings. Frank pointed the nose of the converted Stationair into the wind and revved up the engine.

The plane bounced over the waves as it gained speed, then rose into the late-morning sky.

"Yippee!" said Iola. "So long school, so long books, so long homework! Hello white sand beaches and days with nothing to do but relax!"

The air over the Caribbean was clear and calm as the Hardys charted a course toward San Esteban. To the northeast, though, they all spotted thunderclouds.

"That must be the storm my mom was worried about," said Callie.

Frank shuffled through the papers in the cockpit. "Well, they didn't give us any weather advisories for the flight," he said. "So we should be clear all the way to the island."

"Let's hope that we have clear skies for the whole vacation," Iola said.

"Afternoon showers are common in the Caribbean," Joe commented. "But they usually blow over by evening."

"A good time for a siesta, I'd think," Callie said.

"Or shopping," added Iola.

"We'll have plenty of time for all of that," Frank said. "We've got ten days until we turn this bird around and head home."

The old Stationair soared through the morning sky. Miles of blue-green ocean passed beneath them. Occasionally the teens could make out a fishing boat or a small coral key or a pod of dolphins racing across the water's surface. Mostly, though, they enjoyed the beautiful serenity of sun, sky, and ocean.

"I'm feeling relaxed already," Iola said, leaning back in her seat and closing her eyes.

"Don't get too comfortable," Frank cautioned. "We'll be landing soon. That's San Esteban, dead ahead."

The Hardys and the girls peered through the windshield at the small, mountainous island on the horizon. San Esteban looked like an emerald rising from the turquoise water. Verdant jungles tumbled down the mountain slopes to bright white beaches.

"The town on the south is Nuevo Esteban," Joe said, pointing to a collection of beige buildings near the seaside, at the base of a mountain.

"I wonder if we'll be able to see our bungalows as we near landing," Callie said.

"They're supposed to be pretty secluded," Frank replied. "We might be able to see the main hotel, though."

"It all looks *wonderful*," Iola said, sighing.

10

"I can see the landing strip next to the harbor," Frank said. "Check the regular landing gear, would you, Joe?"

"Roger," the younger Hardy replied. He flicked a switch on the control panel and a light came on. A moment later whirring electric motors extended the wheels below the airplane's pontoons. "Landing gear: check," Joe said.

The plane's engine sputtered.

"What's wrong?" Callie asked.

"I don't know," Frank replied. "We're losing power. Joe, help me out here."

The two brothers began methodically checking controls and throwing switches. Despite their efforts the engine's coughing grew steadily worse.

With a final gasp the engine stopped. The small plane plunged toward the sea.

2 Bull Marketplace

Frank fought desperately to regain control of the stalled airplane.

"Hang on, everyone!" Joe called.

"Can't you land on the water?" Callie asked, her voice shrill with tension. "We have pontoons."

"Having the regular landing gear down will make it tricky," Frank replied. "I think I can pull off an ocean landing if we have to, but . . ." He continued wrestling with the steering yoke as Joe worked the instrument panel, trying to restart the engine.

"I thought Jose said the plane had passed inspection last week!" Iola said, panic creeping into her voice.

"Just stay cool," Joe said. "We're doing everything we can."

Seconds felt like ages as the brothers worked frantically to regain control. Just when they seemed doomed to plunge into the waves, Frank managed to pull the old Stationair's nose up.

"As a glider," he said, sweat pouring down his face, "this plane makes a good boat."

The girls giggled nervously and held on tight to their seats.

The Stationair leveled off at fifteen hundred feet, low enough for the teens to see individual dolphins darting through the white-capped waves below.

"How long can we glide like this?" Callie asked.

"Not long enough to reach the island," Joe replied. He flicked a series of switches and turned to Frank. "Try the engine again."

Frank hit the starter, and the engine sputtered back to life.

The teens let out a collective cheer. Frank moved the plane into a gentle climb, being careful not to stall the engine. He wanted to gain enough altitude so they could glide to their destination if the motor cut out again.

"Is the landing gear still down?" he asked Joe.

Joe nodded. "Do you want me to bring it up again?"

"And take a chance that it might not redeploy? No thanks."

Joe got on the radio and let the control tower know their situation. The small airstrip gave them a priority landing flight path and cleared the area of other traffic.

The teens sat on pins and needles for more than a half hour as Frank and Joe nursed the plane toward San Esteban.

Frank set the plane on final approach, while Joe checked through the systems one last time. "I'm worried about that landing gear," he said. "The light's on, but I can't see the wheels clearly from the window."

"The trouble seemed to start when we hit that switch," Frank said. "There might be some kind of electrical short—but there's nothing we can do about it now. Hang on to your hats, everyone. This landing could be a little rough."

The elder Hardy directed the plane toward the end of the short landing strip. The airport at Nuevo Esteban wasn't very large; it was little more than a patch of flat grass, a few buildings, and a low tower. A fire engine and ambulance stood ready at the side of the field.

All four teens held their breath as the plane dropped slowly toward the ground.

A shudder ran through the Stationair as it touched down. A loud screeching sound filled the air, and the plane tugged suddenly to the left. Frank pulled on the yoke and applied the brake. The plane careened across the runway, heading for the tall grass on the side of the narrow strip.

The plane veered right, responding to Frank's controls. It slowed down quickly as it bumped over the unpaved runway. The engine sputtered and nearly died again as the plane ground to a halt.

Frank, Joe, Callie, and Iola let out a collective sigh of relief. Frank taxied the old plane across the grassy field toward the buildings on the far side of the airport. As they went rescue teams ran out onto the runway. Frank gave the rescue workers the thumbs-up. The workers kept their distance until the plane had stopped near the control tower.

As the teens opened the door a thin, dark-haired man ran up to greet them.

"Are you all right?" he asked. "I am so sorry about this. I am Pablo Ruiz, owner of Ruiz Rentals." The four friends could see the resemblance to his brother, Jose—though Pablo was taller and more handsome.

"We're fine," Joe said.

"Just a few rattled nerves," Callie added.

"I think there might be some kind of short circuit in the landing gear," Frank said. "We didn't have any trouble before throwing the switch to bring it down."

"And the left wheel screeched something awful when we landed," Iola said.

Frank nodded. "The plane pulled that way when we landed, too."

"I'll check right into it," Pablo said.

As the teens and the plane's owner chatted, the rescue service team came and checked the plane. Finding no fires, leaking fuel, or other obvious hazards, they soon packed up their gear and headed for another call.

Pablo scratched his head. "I am very glad none of you were hurt," he said. "But why did you choose to fly *this* aircraft rather than the one the travel agency requested?"

"Jose said the Sullivan Brothers amphibian had engine trouble," Joe replied.

Pablo Ruiz rolled his eyes. "My brother, Jose!" he said. "I wish he would tell me as much as he tells my customers."

"Is he unreliable?" Frank asked.

"He is a very good mechanic," Pablo said, "but not so good behind a desk. Office help is so hard to find around here. I will have a temp working on Kendall Key later today, but until then . . ." He shrugged. "Our assistant quit last week. I hope to hire someone new soon—someone who will call and tell me when problems happen. Jose tells me when it suits him. He will get an earful later tonight." He tried a smile. "Let me help you with your luggage."

Pablo and the Hardys quickly unloaded the plane. The rental owner then checked the landing gear. "It is hard to tell because of the pontoon," he said, "but that wheel definitely looks stuck. I'll have

Jose work on it when he comes back to the island tonight."

"I'm sure your next customers will appreciate it," Joe said.

Pablo frowned. "Please do not go away angry," he said. "Because of this trouble there is no charge for today. I will refund your money to your credit card. Plus I will give you a free afternoon rental of any of our boats or planes, or a free guided tour of your choice."

"That sounds fair," Frank said. "For now, though, I think we need to get to our hotel."

"Can I use your phone?" Iola asked Pablo. "I need to arrange for my cousin to meet us."

"Sure thing," said Pablo. "The phone is on the desk in my office, over there." He pointed to a prefab metal building near the water. A big RUIZ RENTALS sign hung over the door. The building looked somewhat more reputable than the branch office on Kendall Key.

Pablo got in the crippled plane and taxied it to a hangar near his office while Iola went and made the call.

When she returned, she said, "Angela will be here in a couple of minutes. She's coming from her job in the open-air market, and it's not too far from here. The shuttle bus to our hotel leaves from there, too."

"That's convenient," said Joe. He and Frank hefted the heavier travel bags over their shoulders, while

Callie and Iola grabbed the rest. They all walked to the airport's front entrance. A few minutes later a teenager in a long, brightly colored dress and white blouse rode up on a bicycle. She had long, wavy black hair and brown eyes. Her complexion was darker than Iola's or Chet's, but it was still easy to see her resemblance to the Morton family.

"Hi, Cuz!" Iola called to the girl. She stopped next to the teenagers, got off the bike, and gave Iola a hug.

"You must be Angela Martinez," Callie said, shaking the girl's hand. "I'm Callie Shaw, and these are our friends Frank and Joe Hardy."

"The famous Hardy boys," Angela said, a twinkle in her eye. "Iola's written me a lot of e-mails about you two." A friendly Caribbean accent tinged her voice—which sounded very much like Iola's.

Joe grinned and shook Angela's hand. "At least you didn't say *infamous*," he said.

Frank shook hands as well. "We're not really famous," the elder Hardy added.

The warm breeze tossed Angela's wavy hair. "So, Iola, which one is yours?"

"The blond," Iola replied. She gave Joe a quick hug. "Isn't he a hunk?"

"The dark-haired one isn't that bad either," Callie added, putting her arm around Frank's shoulder.

Angela laughed. "We better get going," she said,

"I need to get back to my job. Do you need a hand with your things?"

"We're fine," Frank replied.

Joe adjusted one of the bags on his shoulder. "Unless your job is a long way off," he said.

"No," Angela replied. "Both the marketplace and the shuttle stop are close by. Nothing in Nuevo Esteban is very far. Our city is not very large. Follow me."

The four teens walked out of the airport and through the bustling streets of Nuevo Esteban. They followed Angela as she walked her bike. Most of the people they saw seemed to be local residents going about their daily business. Bicycles, rather than cars, were the main means of transportation. Traffic moved at its own pace, largely without the aid of traffic lights.

None of the buildings they saw were more than two stories high. Most were painted white and had a storefront on the first floor. Colorful hand-painted signs hawking all manner of goods adorned the store windows. Small groups of tourists milled through the streets. Some stopped in the shops and were buying souvenirs and other items unique to the small island. The percentage of sightseers seemed to grow larger as the teens approached the open-air marketplace.

Just as Angela had said, the market wasn't very far from the Ruiz Rentals office. The marketplace occupied the same jutting cape of land as the airstrip, with only a few busy streets in between the two. Brightly colored banners and tentlike stalls occupied nearly every inch of the wide, open square that formed the market. Tourists and local people bustled between the businesses, buying, selling, and trading wares.

"This is quite a place," Iola said, glancing around at all the things for sale.

Nearly everything under the sun seemed to be offered in the market. Clothing, jewelry, fresh food, tourist knickknacks, and even live animals were for sale. Men wearing advertisements on sandwich boards wove through the shoppers. Numerous salespeople loudly hawked their wares, and a white-hatted man seemed to be shaking hands with nearly everyone in the square. The sounds of shopping and music, both live and recorded, filled the air. The peaceful green mountains on the other side of the nearby bay formed a serene backdrop to all the commotion.

"You can find almost anything you want to buy here," Angela said, speaking loudly to make herself heard above the din.

"If you don't get lost looking," Callie observed.

Angela deftly steered the group through the hustle and bustle toward a clothing stall near one side of the square. To the left of the shop stood a pay phone stall. To the right stood a cluster of live-animal retailers. Most sold chickens and other animals. One shop, though, featured a live bull in a large wooden pen. The sign above the pen read EL DIABLO. The bull, a huge, jet-black brute, seemed to deserve his name. He pawed the ground, snorted, and bellowed before pacing around his cage.

"Nice neighbors," Joe said wryly as Angela settled in behind her sales table.

"Every day it's something new," Iola's cousin replied. "Last week it was big snakes. The bull is a nice change. If you want to buy some of our clothing, I can get you a good price." She smiled.

"These things are all lovely!" Callie said, holding up a flower-print skirt.

"I think for now we'd better check in at our hotel," Frank said.

"We'll come shopping later, though," Iola added.

"Which way is it to the shuttle bus stop?" Joe asked.

"Just over there," Angela said, pointing toward the far side of the market. "You can almost see the sign from here. It's right behind the stand that sells the big kites."

"Got it," Frank said. "Thanks. We'll check back with you later."

"Maybe we could go somewhere tonight?" Iola suggested.

"I have to work pretty late," Angela said. "But we'll see."

21

"Thanks again," Joe said.

As the four friends turned to go they bumped into the tall man in a white hat and coat. The man grabbed Iola's hand and shook it. "I'm Jorge Tejeda," he said to a surprised Iola. "I would appreciate your support in the upcoming election."

"B-But I'm just a tourist," Iola said.

"Really?" Tejeda replied in a suave voice. "I thought I had seen you around before." As he glanced over Iola's shoulder his face brightened. "Ah! I see," he said. "You must be visiting your sister."

"Cousin, actually," Joe replied, looking the politician over carefully. Tejeda's white suit was clean and well pressed, his goatee perfectly trimmed. His hands were large and callused, as though he'd spent much of his life working hard with his hands. His dark eyes sparkled. His smile was the practiced grin of someone who'd spent long years wooing constituents.

"Well, young lady," Tejeda said, gazing at Angela, "I hope that *you* will support me." He reached over the table and shook her hand. "And I hope the rest of you will enjoy your stay on our beautiful island," he added to the others.

"Thanks," Frank replied.

Tejeda nodded at them all and slipped back into the crowd, shaking hands as he went.

"Where there's a crowd, there's Tejeda," Angela said as the politician left. "He owns the local cavern tours business, as well as a bunch other local properties. Since he got elected, he's hired someone to run the tours and his other businesses."

"So he's a full-time politician." Joe said.

Angela nodded. "*Sí.* He visits the market at least twice a week just to shake people's hands."

"He seemed nice enough," Callie said.

"Let's get going," Frank said. "We don't want to miss our shuttle." He and the others picked up their bags once again.

As they began to push through the crowd, though, a panicked voice rose above the din.

"Run! Run! El Diablo is loose!"

3 Are We Having Fun Yet?

A deafening collective scream filled the air.

The Hardys and their girlfriends turned as the crowd scattered around them. Less than a dozen yards away stood the great black bull named El Diablo. He pawed the dirt and snorted as people shoved their way out of the square. The door to his pen stood open, the marks of the bull's horns scarring the white-painted wood.

El Diablo focused his bloodshot eyes on the stunned Americans and charged.

Frank and Joe dropped their bags and pushed their girlfriends out of the way as the bull thundered past. The beast passed between them, barely missing the Hardys. The circle of the crowd around the teens grew wider every moment, forming a living bullring, with the four friends trapped in the center.

El Diablo wheeled around, looked at the Hardys, and lowered his head once again. The bull stomped the earth and shook his horns from side to side like a swordsman limbering up.

"Run!" Frank said to Callie and Iola. "We can hold him off until you get away."

"But what about *you*?" Callie asked, fear in her brown eyes.

"We'll be okay," Joe said. "You two get out of here."

"Come on, Callie," Iola said, frantically pulling her friend away from the center of the impromptu arena.

Frank and Joe kept their eyes fixed on El Diablo. The bull snorted and glowered back.

"Some vacation," Joe said quietly to his brother. "Any ideas?"

Frank shook his head.

El Diablo charged. Again Frank and Joe darted out of the way, and the bull passed between them.

"He won't fall for that again," Frank said as the bull wheeled around to face them once more.

"Too bad I left my red cape at home," Joe replied.

"Hey! *Toro!*" called a voice from nearby. El Diablo turned toward the sound.

Standing near the edge of the crowd was a young man with short, curly black hair. He wore jeans and a black T-shirt. In his outstretched hands he held a ragged jean jacket. He waved the jacket like a matador's cape. "Hey, *toro!*" he repeated.

"Hey, *toro!*" said another voice. The Hardys turned and saw Jorge Tejeda with his jacket off as well. The politician waved his white coat at the enraged animal.

The bull glanced from the Hardys to the two mock matadors, unable to decide whom to charge.

"These guys have the right idea," Joe said. "Too bad we're not wearing jackets."

"I think it's the movement that attracts the bull, not the cape," Frank said.

Joe's blue eyes gleamed. "Let's find out," he said. Raising his arms, he stepped farther away from Frank and shouted, "Hey, *toro!*"

Frank stepped in the opposite direction, yelling, "Hey, bull! Hey, bull!"

Confused, the animal stamped the ground, glancing from man to man. He turned in circles, trying to find the best opponent.

The teen with the jean jacket jumped close to the beast, waving his "cape" in the bull's face. The bull lunged at him, but he danced back out of the way.

"Hey, Frank, I've got an idea," Joe said. "Follow my lead and be ready to close that gate."

As Frank nodded the younger Hardy stripped off his T-shirt and moved closer to the enraged animal. "Yo! *Toro!*" he called, placing himself between El Diablo and the bull's pen.

The bull turned away from the jean-clad youth,

who had danced farther out of the way, and focused on Joe.

The younger Hardy backed toward the open pen, waving his shirt and saying, *"Toro! Toro! Toro!"*

The bull charged. Joe turned and sprinted toward the pen, El Diablo in hot pursuit. Frank realized what Joe was doing, and ran toward the side of the pen where the gate stood open.

"Crazy *Americano!*" shouted Jorge Tejeda as the bull closed in on Joe.

Joe could almost feel El Diablo's hot breath on his back as he ran into the pen. He didn't dare look back; the enraged beast might catch him if he did. He heard an angry snort and the animal's hooves thundering closer.

At the last second Joe threw himself sideways, vaulting over the pen's fence.

El Diablo bellowed with rage, having lost his victim. Frank slammed the gate shut behind the bull, trapping El Diablo in the pen.

A cheer went up from the crowd as the elder Hardy raced to his brother's side. "Are you okay, Joe?" he asked.

Joe got up and dusted himself off. "Good thing I like to high-jump," he said, grinning broadly. As he put his shirt back on, Iola and Callie raced up and gave both brothers a hug.

"The way I see it," said a hawk-faced man standing nearby, "you boys have done *two* foolish things

27

this morning." He pushed through the crowd that had gathered around the pen, and stood next to the brothers. His skin was tan and weathered like old leather. About four days' growth of salt-and-pepper beard decorated his chin. The humid island breeze made the man's long, stringy gray hair dance around his face. His blue eyes flashed brightly.

"What do you mean?" Joe asked, annoyed.

"Toying with the bull was bad enough," the man said. "But you also took the limelight away from Jamie Escobar. That's doubly dangerous."

"Who's Jamie Escobar?" Frank asked. "And who are you?"

"My name is Lucas McGill," the man said, "though most people know me as The Gringo." He smiled and his face turned into a mass of leathery wrinkles. "As for Escobar, he's the young guy in the jean jacket."

The Hardys and their girlfriends looked at the teen who had first confronted the bull. Though he was surrounded by a crowd admiring his bravery, Jamie Escobar didn't look too pleased.

Nearby Jorge Tejeda had gone back to shaking hands. He paused just long enough to wipe the sweat from his forehead and put on his white jacket once more. Then he went back to socializing.

"Tejeda may get a bump in the polls from this," The Gringo said wryly. "Politicians are always looking for ways to be seen as heroes. Riling Escobar, though . . . that could make your stay on San Este-ban . . . unpleasant."

"What does it matter to you?" Joe asked suspi-ciously.

The Gringo winked. "We Americans have to stick together down here," he said. "Keep out of the way of the locals. They play rough."

"Thanks for the warning," Frank said. "We're not looking for any trouble."

"In San Esteban trouble finds you," The Gringo replied. He turned and vanished back into the crowd as quickly as he'd come.

"What a strange man," Callie said, trying to sup-press a shudder.

With the excitement over, the crowd returned to their business. As the others left Angela pushed her way to her cousin's side.

"Are any of you hurt?" she asked.

"We're all fine," Iola replied.

"Though not for lack of trying," Callie added, giving the brothers a reprimanding look.

"Don't worry," Frank said, "no more bull wran-gling for us."

"Well," Angela said, "since you're okay, I should get back to work. Call me when you get a chance."

"We'll need some downtime first," Iola said. "But we'll definitely call."

Angela went back to her booth, and the Bayport teens all took a moment to catch their breath.

29

"Make sure this pen doesn't get open again," Frank said to the short, dark-haired man tending El Diablo.

"*Sí, señor,*" the man replied, bowing slightly. "I am very sorry for the trouble. I cannot imagine how it happened."

The brothers and their girlfriends gathered their luggage and walked toward the shuttle bus stop.

"That's enough excitement for this vacation, thank you very much," Iola remarked. She gave the brothers a weary half smile.

"Next time," Joe said, "tell the bull." He gave her a reassuring hug and then pointed to a towering, coral-colored building across the bay. "Do you think that's our hotel?"

Callie shook her head. "According to the literature, the Casa Bonita is farther up the coast," she said.

"That has to be the Hotel San Esteban," Iola added. "It's supposed to be the biggest building in Nuevo Esteban. We thought about booking there, but you should see the rates!"

"They must be something," Frank said, "considering what we're paying already."

"Believe me," Callie said, "Casa Bonita is a much better deal. The rates are cheaper and not bad— after all, we've got private bungalows near the water."

"I'm all for that," Joe said. "I could already use some peace and quiet."

They got to the bus stop just a few minutes before the bus arrived. Rather than a sleek, modern vehicle, the Casa Bonita shuttle was a renovated school bus, painted white, with blue-and-green decorations and lettering.

The Hardys and their girlfriends climbed onto the bus, stowed their luggage in the overhead racks, and sat back to enjoy the ride. The rickety shuttle wound through the crowded streets and then down the narrow highway toward the north coast. They soon passed the large coral building, which, sure enough, had a big HOTEL SAN ESTEBAN sign in front of it.

They caught a glimpse of a long, white-sand beach beyond the hotel. A number of small, cabin-like bungalows peeked through the palm trees lining the coast. They passed over a wide, swift-moving river and a few minutes later pulled up in front of Casa Bonita.

This hotel was not nearly as large or impressive as the Hotel San Esteban. The architecture was from an older period, and the building looked slightly dingy, despite new coats of white, blue, and green paint. Still, it was close to the waterfront, and it had a nice view of the green mountains and the cliffs to the north.

"The beach is the same one that runs past the Hotel San Esteban," Iola said. "Though the river divides it in the middle."

31

"The hotels share the breakwater to the north and the recreation facilities in between," Callie explained. "All the bungalows south of here belong to the Hotel San Esteban. Water taxis shuttle their guests up the coast."

"So our bungalows are to the north, then?" Frank asked.

Callie nodded. "They have a beautiful view," she said, "but we'll have to come back here for swimming."

"Unless you're into cliff diving," Iola added.

Joe and Frank smiled at each other. "That could work," Joe said.

"It worked for Elvis Presley," Frank agreed.

"Though he probably had a stunt double," Joe concluded.

"I do *not* want to spend my vacation waiting in the emergency room!" Callie said, smiling. "There are plenty of less dangerous sports you two can try while we're here."

Iola looped her arm around Joe's. "Let's check in before these two think of any, hmm?" she said.

The four teens registered at Casa Bonita's desk and got the keys to their cabins. The girl behind the counter couldn't locate their rental car, so they had to talk with the hotel's owner and manager, Renee Aranya.

Aranya was a short, thin, middle-aged woman with frizzy brown hair and hazel eyes. She quickly turned up the Jeep reserved for the vacationers from Bayport.

"I'm sorry for the trouble," Aranya said, "but things have been so hectic around here lately!" She helped load the teens' luggage into the back of the Jeep. "Is there anything else I can help with?"

"We'll call if we need anything," Frank said.

Aranya's face fell. "Y-You can't," she said. "Your bungalows don't have phones. Our literature was very specific on that point. Cell phones don't work on this part of the island either." She shrugged. "We're not 'wired' yet. I'm very sorry."

"That's all right," Callie said.

Aranya smiled wanly. "I'm so glad you understand." She handed them a piece of paper. "Here's the map to the cabins. It's a very beautiful drive."

"I'm sure it is," Frank said, taking the map.

"Please feel free to enjoy the hotel beach and our resort's other facilities," Aranya said.

"We'll probably do so this afternoon," Iola replied.

Aranya nodded. "Very good. We'll see you soon, then." She bustled back into the office as the teens all piled into the Jeep.

They drove north along the narrow road, following the directions on the map that Aranya had given them. The drive to the bungalows was beautiful, but it was also longer than they expected. The road wound through dense, junglelike forests and up the hillside. The path grew progressively more rutted and rocky as they went. By the time they reached their destination, they were all feeling *very* alone.

Two quaint bungalows stood in the small clearing on top of the cliff. The cabins were almost Hawaiian looking, with thatched roofs and walls, and bamboo supports and beams. The buildings seemed in good repair, and both boasted spectacular views of the sea.

Callie frowned, eyeing the dark thunderheads approaching from the northeast. "Shoot!" she said. "Mom may have been right about that storm."

Iola put her arm around Callie's shoulder. "Worry-wart!" she said. "We're not going to let a little rain spoil our vacation, are we?"

Callie laughed and shook her head. "You're right. The worrying stops now. Come on, let's stash our bags and change into our swimsuits. We can hit the hotel beach before the storm catches up with us."

"Sounds like a plan," Frank replied.

The Hardys put their bags in one cabin, and the girls took the other. Despite their rustic appearance, the bungalows had modern conveniences inside. Because no power lines ran up the cliff, each cabin sported a set of solar panels on the south roofline and, in the back, a wooden box—about the size of a sideways refrigerator—filled with storage batteries.

"Not too bad," Frank said as they stowed their towels and other gear in the Jeep for the trip down-hill.

"After the hustle and bustle of Bayport, I think this is just what the doctor ordered," Joe agreed.

They all climbed into the Jeep, and twenty minutes later they were lounging in the late-afternoon sunshine on the beach in front of the Casa Bonita.

"Now, this is more like it," Callie said, sighing. She stretched, closed her eyes, and lay back on her beach towel. Adjusting her sunglasses, Iola did the same on the towel next to her friend.

"Want to toss the Frisbee around, Joe?" Frank asked. He'd picked up a flying disk from the hotel's recreational equipment shack before hitting the beach.

"Maybe later," Joe replied. "I want to take a dip first."

"Sounds good," Frank said. The Hardys hiked down the beach toward the surf.

As they did a shriek cut through the afternoon air. "Help! Help!" It was a woman's voice.

A short distance up the beach a sleek powerboat lay anchored by the breakwater. Inside the boat the Hardys spotted a woman in a one-piece bathing suit struggling with two black-masked men. Before the Hardys could do anything, the masked men dumped the woman overboard.

4 Wave Runners

The woman fell hard, but she quickly bobbed to the surface, sputtering and coughing. The Hardys and their girlfriends sprinted up the beach toward her. The beach wasn't very crowded, and most of the vacationers were concentrated to the south, closer to the big hotel. The Bayport teens were the only ones in a position to help.

The two attackers sat down and fired up the powerboat's engine while their victim struggled in the water. Black nylon masks obscured the men's features, making them impossible to recognize.

"Help the woman!" Frank shouted to Callie and Iola as they ran.

"We'll go after the attackers," Joe concluded.

"Check!" Iola called. She and Callie splashed into

the surf and swam toward the floundering victim.

The brothers kept running up the beach. As they neared the scene the boat turned in a circle and headed out to sea.

"We'll never catch them!" Joe said, frustration burning in his voice.

"We're not licked yet," Frank said. "They have to pass the breakwater to get out of the bay."

Joe nodded, and the two of them rocketed off the beach and down the breakwater. Concrete, large rocks, and small boulders formed the base of the causeway, which had a concrete walkway for fishing along the top. The breakwater stretched out into the bay like a stony finger, protecting the hotel beaches from the ravages of the open ocean.

The cement walkway was rough and weathered. Its hot surface stung the Hardys' bare feet as they ran down it, trying to head off the stolen boat. The attackers hadn't noticed them yet, which gave the brothers an advantage.

The Hardys reached the end of the breakwater at the same time as the stolen boat. Frank and Joe sprang off the causeway with all their might and angled out over the rocks. They landed hard in the middle of the speedboat between the two bandits.

The two men spun to meet their followers. The man in the rear of the boat grabbed an oar and swung it at Frank's head. Frank ducked out of the way and aimed a low kick at the man's knee, but the boat lurched over a wave and Frank missed.

Joe moved forward to grapple with the driver of the boat. The man spun the wheel hard, and Joe toppled against the ship's fiberglass hull. Joe staggered to his feet and lunged again. The driver was ready, though, and kicked Joe in the jaw. The younger Hardy fell hard to the deck, spots dancing before his eyes.

The man in the back of the boat steadied himself for another swing at Frank. The older Hardy sprang up and grabbed the oar with both hands. He forced the culprit back against the stern rail, near the outboard motor. The two wrestled, each trying to twist the oar from the other's hands. Frank brought his knee up into the man's thigh. The man gasped and Frank pushed hard, clouting the bandit on the chin with the oar. Stunned, the bandit lost his grip on the paddle and slumped to the deck.

At the front of the craft Joe quickly got to his feet for another go at the driver. The pirate at the controls gave three quick twists of the wheel. Still slightly dazed, the younger Hardy swayed on his feet. The boat's final turn sent him tumbling toward the sea.

Frank realized his brother's predicament and thrust one end of the oar toward Joe. Joe grabbed it just as the boat driver executed a high-speed turn.

Joe and Frank held tight to either end of the oar, but both lost their footing on the boat. The brothers tumbled into the surf. They popped quickly to the surface as the craft zipped away into the open ocean.

"Are you all right?" Frank asked, spitting out seawater.

Joe nodded. "I've been better," he said. "Man! We came so close to catching those guys!"

Currents near the breakwater made returning to the causeway dangerous, so the brothers swam all the way back to the beach. When they got there, they found a crowd of people gathered around their girlfriends and the rescued woman.

The local sheriff was taking notes while talking to the victim: a middle-aged blond woman named Beth Becker. Renee Aranya stood nearby, arguing with a distinguished-looking man. Lucas McGill, dressed like a beachcomber, lurked at the edges of the crowd. He gave the Hardys a thumbs-up sign and a wink as they staggered out of the water.

Callie and Iola helped the brothers to some nearby beach chairs. "Are you okay?" Callie asked.

"Just peachy," Joe said, still angry that the pirates had gotten away.

"It's not quite the swim I planned for this afternoon . . . ," Frank admitted.

The girls gave the brothers a quick hug. "Heroic, but foolish," Iola said. Callie nodded and frowned.

A dune buggy screeched out of the Casa Bonita parking lot and moved quickly down the beach. It stopped right next to the crowd. Pablo Ruiz hopped out and ran over to Beth Becker. He looked very worried.

"Ms. Becker," he said, "are you all right?"

"Do I look all right?" Ms. Becker snapped. "I was hijacked and dumped overboard!"

"But you are not injured?" Pablo asked.

Beth Becker rubbed her neck. "They were pretty rough," she said. "I doubt I'll recover before flying home. Some vacation this is!"

Pablo gave Ms. Becker a sympathetic look. "And . . . my boat?"

"Stolen," Frank interjected. "They headed north, out to sea."

"Frank and I tried to stop them," Joe continued, "but they threw us overboard too."

"Lucky for you," the sheriff said. He was a stocky, powerful-looking man wearing a khaki uniform and dark glasses. "The local pirates are ruthless. You could have been killed."

Pablo rubbed his head. "First the airplane trouble, now this!" he said, moaning.

"Honestly," Ms. Becker said, raising her voice once more, "this is inexcusable! People told me there'd been problems locally. Someone should be held accountable. I'm thinking of filing a lawsuit."

At the word *lawsuit*, Renee Aranya and the man she was arguing with suddenly stopped talking.

"This is your fault," the man hissed to Aranya. "Your sloppy management is hurting my business.

Now this woman talks of suing someone. Well, it won't be me!"

"Your hotel manages this beach too, Rodrigo," Aranya said angrily. "Those aren't *my* bungalows south of Casa Bonita. Whether you like it or not, Señor Lopez, Casa Bonita and the Hotel San Esteban are in this together."

"Everyone, please, calm down," the sheriff said. "There is no need for lawsuits, nor any reason to cast blame on one another. Clearly neither Ms. Aranya nor Mr. Lopez is responsible for these pirates."

"Well, *someone's* got to take charge," Beth Becker complained.

"The sheriff looks in charge to me," Frank said.

"We should let him do his job," Joe added.

Ms. Becker seemed to notice the Bayport teens for the first time. She smiled weakly. "I suppose you're right," she said. "I'm just upset. I haven't even thanked you four for saving me."

"No trouble," Iola said.

"You'd have done the same for us," Callie added.

Ms. Becker nodded. The look on her face, however, told the teens that she wouldn't have been so brave.

"Remaining calm will make the investigation much easier," the sheriff said. "Now, I will require a statement from each of you. . . ."

It was almost sunset by the time the Hardys,

their girlfriends, and the other people had finished talking to the police. Deputies spoke to everyone who might have witnessed the incident, including the hotels' guests and other beachgoers. The questioning left the four Bayport teens exhausted.

"I'll call Angela and tell her we're too tired to party tonight," Iola said, heading for the hotel lobby to make the call.

"Good idea," Callie agreed. She and the Hardys gathered their towels and other beach gear. As they did Lucas McGill, who had been hanging around the fringes of the crowd, sauntered up.

"You didn't follow my advice," The Gringo said.

"Which advice was that?" Joe asked, a bit peeved.

"About staying out of the way of the locals," McGill replied. "You haven't even been here one day, and already you've tangled with a mad bull, a young tough guy, and some pirates. Your vacation could be cut short if you don't wise up."

Frank ignored the implied warning. "That man arguing with Ms. Aranya," he said. "Is he the owner of the Hotel San Esteban?"

"Yes," The Gringo replied. "Rodrigo Lopez is one of the most powerful men on the island. You should *especially* stay out of his way." McGill cracked a half smile. "Well, I'm sure you'll be wanting to get back to your cabins." He turned and walked down the beach toward the larger hotel. "Remember what I've said," he called back. "Keep your noses clean."

Joe scratched his head. "What do you make of that guy?" he asked Frank and Callie.

Both of them shrugged. "He's not just a friendly beachcomber," Frank said. "But I have no idea what his game might be."

"*Please* don't turn this vacation into a detective case," Callie pleaded. "Can't some people just be eccentric?"

Frank rubbed his chin and nodded.

Iola returned a few minutes later looking a bit forlorn.

"What's wrong?" Joe asked.

"The weather forecast," she said, sighing. "Callie's mom may have been right about that storm. It's a hurricane now, and it's heading this way."

"Well, we can't control the storm," Frank said. "We may as well enjoy ourselves and see what happens."

"Hear, hear," said Callie.

The sun set while they finished packing their gear into the Jeep. They grabbed some sandwiches from the hotel's tiny beachside café for dinner. They ate in the car, and by the time they got back to their cabins, they all felt exhausted.

"I hope you don't mind calling it a day this early," Callie said, giving Frank a peck on the cheek.

"Nah," the elder Hardy said. "I'm beat."

"Me too," agreed Joe.

"We'll see you in the morning, then," Iola said, giving Joe a quick hug. "Bright and early."

"Not *too* early," the younger Hardy said.

Iola and Callie went into their cabin, and the brothers headed for theirs. At the door Frank paused and frowned.

"Didn't we latch this screen before we left?" he asked.

"I *thought* we did," Joe replied. "But we were rushing to hit the beach." He shrugged. "So, who knows?"

They entered the bungalow cautiously, listening for a moment before turning on the lights. Nothing seemed amiss, so they flicked on the light switch. They'd unpacked their swimsuits, but nothing else seemed to be missing from their bags.

"No missing credit cards or traveler's checks," Frank said.

"Our watches are here too," Joe said. "We must have forgotten to latch the screen. I'm gonna take a shower and then turn in."

Frank nodded. "I'll unpack and then shower when you're done."

"Fair enough," Joe said. Fifteen minutes later he and Frank had switched places. The elder Hardy washed while Joe unpacked the last of his clothes into the cabin's rustic chest of drawers.

The younger Hardy took a long, deep breath before flouncing back onto his twin bed. The bed was made of bamboo, and it had a single warm blanket on top with a sheet underneath. "Now the vacation *really* begins," he muttered to himself.

Joe crawled under the covers, lay on his back, and closed his eyes. He could hear Frank finishing his shower. Outside the ocean breeze whispered gently, and the surf hissed against the rocks.

Joe sighed and began to drift gently into sleep.

For a moment the younger Hardy thought he was just imagining something moving under the covers.

Then it moved again.

Joe opened his eyes and looked cautiously around the room. Frank had come out of the bathroom and was standing near the dresser, buttoning the top of his pajama pants.

"Frank?" Joe said.

"Yeah?" Frank replied without looking. He fished his toothbrush out of his shaving kit.

"I think there's something else under these sheets." Joe flipped the sheet off the bed, and his blood ran cold with the sight he took in.

Crawling up his right calf was a giant spider.

5 Bugged

The tarantula was more than six inches in diameter and reddish brown in color. The fur on its body shivered and its sharp mandibles gnashed as it methodically crept up Joe's leg.

"Frank!" Joe hissed.

"I see it," Frank replied. "Don't move." He pulled a T-shirt out of his dresser drawer and walked cautiously over to Joe's bed.

The arachnid reached Joe's knee and paused. Joe tried to keep from shaking. "Frank!" he hissed again.

Frank nodded, all his attention concentrated on the spider. He held the T-shirt out, as though he might net the creepy invader. Joe shook his head slightly.

"Don't worry," Frank whispered. "I know what I'm doing."

Cautiously he draped the T-shirt down in front of the arachnid.

The tarantula paused again when its front legs hit the cotton fabric. Then it continued creeping toward Joe's torso.

Frank waited until the spider's whole body was on the T-shirt. Then he snatched the fabric up, netting the tarantula inside. He raced to the door, hastily opened the screen, and flicked the creature outside into the bushes.

Joe sighed with relief. "Thanks, Frank," he said.

"No problem," Frank replied. "Let's check that there aren't any more where that came from."

As he said it a shriek pierced the night air.

"The girls!" Joe said.

The Hardys dashed out of their cabin and into the bungalow next door. They found Callie in her nightgown and Iola wrapped in a towel, standing next to the door.

"It's in the tub!" Iola said, pointing toward the bathroom.

The brothers raced inside and threw back the shower curtain. A giant centipede lurked at the bottom of the tub.

"Two unwanted visitors in one night," Frank said.

"What do you mean?" Callie asked. She and Iola

had come to stand in the bathroom doorway behind the brothers.

"I found a tarantula in my bed," Joe replied.

"Ew!" the girls said simultaneously.

"Frank, grab a stick from outside," Joe said. "Iola, get me the wastebasket liner from the other room."

Both Frank and Iola returned a moment later with the things Joe had asked for. Joe had Frank hold the plastic trash bag open near one end of the tub, then prodded the centipede into it with the stick.

Frank scooped up the bug and deposited it outside in the jungle.

"Here's where it got in," Joe said, pointing to one edge of the bathroom window, where the screen had been pushed in slightly. He resealed the screen, and then all of them thoroughly searched both cabins. They turned up no more unwanted visitors.

"I'm going to have nightmares tonight," Iola declared.

"This whole *day* has been a nightmare," Callie said. "We really should complain to the hotel about this."

"With no working phones available, we'll have to wait until morning to do it," Frank noted.

"Unless you want to drive to Casa Bonita tonight," Joe said.

"All I want to do is sleep," Callie said.

"Ditto," added Iola.

"Obviously we need to lock the cabins up tight whenever we leave," Frank said.

"We'll be extra sure about that from now on," Callie said.

Joe nodded. "Well, good night. We'll see you in the morning."

"Pleasant dreams," Frank added with a wink.

Callie threw a pillow at him as he ducked out the door.

The brothers returned to their cabin, latched the door and all the screens, then turned off the lights and went to bed.

"Frank," Joe said just before they dozed off, "it's pretty odd that there were creatures in both cabins."

Frank shrugged. "Maybe the local bugs are very aggressive."

"Maybe," Joe agreed, "but I was sure we locked that screen door before we left this afternoon."

"I thought we did too."

Eventually the brothers drifted off into a fitful sleep.

They woke just after sunrise the next morning, feeling surprisingly refreshed considering their adventures the day before. The rooms had small coffee machines, and the teens took advantage of them before heading outside to check the weather.

Unfortunately dark storm clouds had drawn significantly closer to the island during the night.

Callie frowned. "Let's see if we can squeeze in some beach time before the storm hits," she said.

The four teens packed up their swimsuits and some gear and took the Jeep down to the Casa Bonita beach. They stopped briefly at the hotel desk to complain about their bug problem. Renee Aranya apologized to them personally and offered to give them an extra day's free lodging. The teens' flight home was already scheduled, though, so Aranya promised not to charge them for the previous day.

The four friends changed into their swimsuits at the hotel beach house and picked up some breakfast at the seaside café. Then they headed to the beach to catch a few rays before the clouds rolled in.

They went swimming, though the water had grown colder and turned a cloudy gray overnight, and then lounged until the sun disappeared behind the clouds. As the waves kicked up and rain seemed imminent they sat under the cafe's thatched awning and ate an early lunch. The café was about the size of a gas station kiosk, with an oval bar in the middle and a grill in the center of the bar. Stools were arranged around the outside of the oval, and the bartender-chef worked the inside.

Beth Becker sat nearby, talking loudly to anyone who would listen. Clearly she was still annoyed about the theft of her rented boat the previous day.

"The authorities aren't doing anything," Ms. Becker said to Callie as she walked by. "Do you see them doing anything? Are they combing the beach for clues? Have they arrested anyone?"

"I'm sure they're doing the best they can," Callie replied.

"These things take time," Frank said. "All the beachgoers tramping down the sand would make finding clues on the beach impossible."

"It'd be like looking for a needle in a haystack," Joe added.

Ms. Becker frowned. Clearly she didn't expect anyone to disagree with her—not even in the mildest way. "This isn't the only trouble they've had down here recently, you know," she said. "A bull escaped in the marketplace yesterday, and two days before, some tourists were robbed at gunpoint. There have been suspicious fires, too."

"*Turistas* should learn to stay out of places they're not wanted," said a voice from the other side of the cabana. Jamie Escobar leaned against the bar and sipped a cola. He grinned at the Hardys. "Eh, hombres?"

Frank and Joe ignored him.

"Islands that can't take care of tourists don't deserve any," Ms. Becker continued. "Diffident hotel staff, tiny rooms, robbers, pirates, wild animals in the streets . . . and now this hurricane! Why does *anyone* come here?"

Escobar shook his head and made a *tsk* sound. "You got it rough here, *chica*," he said. "Maybe you

51

should go back to your palace on the mainland."

"Maybe *you* should crawl back into whatever hole you crawled out of," Joe said, glaring.

"Whoo! The boy is *tough*!" Escobar said sarcastically.

"Take it easy, Joe," Frank whispered to his brother. "We don't need to mix it up with this jerk."

"I heard that, hombre!" Escobar said. "And I'll remember it!" He finished his cola and slammed the glass down on the bar. "You *turistas* better watch your step." He stalked out of the cabana and down the beach toward the river.

"See! That's the kind of thing I'm talking about," Ms. Becker said. "Why do they let people like that live around here?"

"I don't think the police can lock someone up for being a jerk," Iola said.

Ms. Becker frowned as rain began to gently fall outside the café. "Don't take my word for it," she said. "Nuevo Esteban is in trouble. There's a town meeting about the problems at noon today."

"Are you going?" Joe asked.

"What's the point?" Ms. Becker said. "Complaining doesn't help in countries like this. I'm going back to my room." She finished her drink and headed back toward Casa Bonita.

Callie shook her head. "Well, at least she's maintaining a positive attitude," she said with a sarcastic smile.

The Hardys and Iola laughed quietly and watched the rain drip down the thatched eaves.

"Let's check out that meeting," Frank said.

"You think there's a pattern to all this trouble?" Callie asked.

"Creatures in both bungalows at the same time," Joe said, "seems like more than coincidence."

"That's *not* what you said last night," Iola replied.

"We didn't want you worrying," Joe said. "But Frank and I were pretty sure we latched our screen door before we left. It was open when we came back."

"Nothing was stolen," Frank said, "but it's still odd. So let's see what comes up at this meeting."

Callie stuck her hand out into the rain. She sighed. "With weather like this," she said, "I suppose we don't have anything better to do."

"If it gets boring," Iola said, "we can always go shopping."

They changed out of their suits and packed their stuff into the Jeep. Then they drove over the bridge and back into the main part of town.

The Nuevo Escobar town hall was similar to most of the city's other buildings. It was two stories tall and constructed in a traditional Spanish style, with a red tile roof and stucco exterior.

The rain started to come down hard as the teens parked and made their way to the meeting. The hall's interior was similar to that of a church, with a high ceiling supported by massive timbers. Electric lights had replaced the traditional chandeliers, but the building was clearly very old. Local residents crowded the floor. Some were standing and talking to one another, while others were sitting on folding chairs. A balcony at the back of the hall provided additional seating.

The Hardys spotted some people they'd met since coming to the island. Renee Aranya was there, speaking quietly to the sheriff. Jorge Tejeda moved deftly through the room, shaking hands whenever he could. Rodrigo Lopez, the owner of the Hotel San Esteban, prowled the edges of the meeting hall, occasionally stopping to talk with someone. The brothers saw Lucas McGill, The Gringo, standing near the back, keeping an eye on the proceedings.

The four teens found seats on one side of the hall just as the mayor took the podium. She was a short, fat woman, well dressed, with black-and-silver hair. She took her gavel and banged it on the podium to bring the meeting to order.

As she did a loud cracking noise shook the meeting hall.

Everyone stopped talking, looking for the source of the sound.

With another loud *crack* and a rumbling groan, the balcony at the back of the hall began to collapse.

6 Storm Winds Blowing

Chaos erupted within the ancient town hall. People ran pell-mell toward the exits, not heeding that the main exit was beneath the collapsing balcony.

"Stay calm!" Frank shouted, but no one was listening. The Hardys, Callie, and Iola pressed themselves against the nearest wall, out of the way of the rushing crowd.

With a final *crack*, one of the balcony's support pillars broke in half. The whole structure slumped to one side, spilling frightened people toward the lower floor. Huge clouds of plaster dust filled the air, and the lights flickered off throughout the building. Everywhere people were screaming and crying.

"Are you all right?" Joe asked the girls. Callie and Iola nodded, though they looked frightened.

"Let's help out if we can," Frank said. "I think the worst of it is over."

They moved quickly across the rubble to where the balcony now lay. Fortunately no one had been pinned by the structure. Many people, though, had been hit with falling debris. The brothers and their friends quickly dug several people out; all had only superficial injuries.

Tejeda quickly organized some of the men into a work crew and began evacuating the injured outside. Rodrigo Lopez pitched in, along with the four Bayport teens. Working together, the rescuers quickly emptied the hall of wounded people. They left the rubble to be cleared later on.

Outside, people who had been at the meeting were still standing around talking, despite the weather. They made way for emergency workers and ambulances, but otherwise stayed clustered together.

Joe, Frank, Callie, and Iola brushed the dust off their clothing.

"It's really lucky no one was badly hurt . . . or killed," Frank said.

"What do you suppose caused the collapse?" Iola asked.

"I would like to know that too," said Rodrigo Lopez.

"I can tell you," said a gangly man dressed in overalls and a carpenter's apron. He had been among those helping out.

"Who's he?" Callie whispered.

"His name is Luis," Lopez said. "He is the handyman who works in the local government offices." Turning to Luis, Lopez asked, "What caused this misfortune?"

The crowd went silent and waited for the handyman's conclusion.

"Termites," Luis pronounced. "I have looked at the broken support beam, and there is evidence termites have eaten through it."

"You see?" Lopez said loudly. "*This* is the kind of trouble I was talking about. This is why I urged we have this meeting. The infrastructure of Nuevo Esteban is crumbling—literally!"

Many in the crowd mumbled their agreement.

"It is no wonder that tourism is declining almost as fast as our property values," Lopez continued, sounding more like a politician than a hotel owner. "We must tell the government that more support is needed! If our current leaders will not do this, we must elect new ones!"

Again the crowd mumbled its assent. No one even seemed to notice the rain anymore.

"Things are not so dark as Señor Lopez paints them," Jorge Tejeda said, stepping to the front of the crowd. "Our people are honest and hardworking; our island is strong."

"*Sí. Sí.* Representative Tejeda is right," agreed the mayor. "Yes, we have problems, but working together, we can solve them. Wailing about our troubles will not help Nuevo Esteban's tourism."

"It's your job to build up this city's reputation, Señor Tejeda," Lopez countered. "But our jobs"—he turned, sweeping his hand toward the crowd—"depend on people actually visiting Nuevo Esteban. No matter what you say, people will *not* come unless our city is a safe, modern place."

"Some people think," another voice interjected, "that you have taken modernism too far, Señor Lopez." The voice belonged to Renee Aranya, who was standing near the back of the gathering. "Who will come to San Esteban if our island has the same hotel chains, the same restaurants, and the same attractions as the mainland and everywhere else? You knocked down a classic island resort to build your modern hotel. Now you are shipping your profits to an offshore bank account. How are you planning on helping our island?"

Rodrigo Lopez turned red. "I have spent a fortune building on this island," he said angrily. "I have a right to make a profit. Who are you to judge me, Renee? Your hotel is hanging on by its fingertips."

"Flinging recriminations won't get you anywhere," Frank interjected. "You all have to pull together."

"What do *you* know, *turista*?" called someone in the crowd.

"We're just trying to help," Joe said.

"We don't need your help," another person

shouted. "We islanders can take care of this ourselves."

A number of young men in the crowd began to jostle the Hardys and their friends. It looked to Frank and Joe as if these were the same kids they'd seen hanging around with Jamie Escobar. Escobar himself, though, was nowhere to be seen. Before things could get ugly, Jorge Tejeda spoke.

"What are you punks doing?" he said, glaring at the young men. "This is exactly the kind of behavior our island does not need."

"Tejeda is right," Renee Aranya said. "We should welcome input from anyone if it will help us solve our problems."

The soaked crowd mumbled their general agreement, and the young men slipped away. The Hardys and their girlfriends let out sighs of relief.

"We need to continue this meeting," Tejeda said, "as soon as the weather is better. Tomorrow, perhaps?"

"But where shall we meet?" the mayor asked. "The chamber of commerce office is too small, and we clearly cannot meet at the town hall."

"I volunteer the ballroom at Casa Bonita," Aranya said. "Everyone will be welcome." Here she looked pointedly at Rodrigo Lopez. The rival hotel owner nodded grudgingly.

"Tomorrow, then," Tejeda said.

"Shall we say noon?" the mayor asked. She gave

her best publicity-photo smile. The people standing in the rain in front of the dilapidated town hall agreed.

"Weather permitting, of course" Aranya said.

The rescheduling of the meeting seemed to satisfy the crowd. With the place and time settled, everyone quickly hustled to get out of the rain.

Frank, Joe, Iola, and Callie sought refuge under the awning in front of a nearby store. People hurriedly passed them on the street carrying storm supplies, like lanterns, bags of groceries, and boards for securing windows against the coming storm.

"I warned you to stay out of it," said a gruff voice from behind them, "but you wouldn't listen."

The four teens turned and saw The Gringo, skulking in the shadows, smoking a cigarette.

"You seem oddly amused by all this," Joe said, his temper rising.

"When you've lived away from America as long as I have," The Gringo said, "you get used to being an outsider."

"But we should still try to help one another, Mr. McGill," Callie said.

The Gringo shrugged and flicked the butt of his cigarette into the rain-clogged gutter. "That'll only bring you heartache, girlie. Take my advice: Keep to yourselves. Stay out of things you don't understand." He turned away, pulled the collar of his raincoat up, and walked off into the rain.

"For someone who keeps telling us to mind our own business," Joe said, "he seems mighty interested in minding *our* business."

Frank nodded. "I still can't figure out what his angle is, though."

"Maybe he *is* just looking out for fellow Americans," Iola said.

The teens all looked at one another and laughed.

"I'll call Angela," Iola suggested. "Maybe we can meet her for an early dinner or something."

"Sounds good," replied Joe. "I don't think we'll be doing any sunbathing this afternoon."

They found a local store with a public phone. The guys bought travel umbrellas while the girls called Iola's cousin. The foldable umbrellas provided only a bit of protection against the weather but kept a little rain off them until they got back to the Jeep.

They saw few tourists on their way to the restaurant Angela had chosen. Huge puddles filled Nuevo Esteban's rutted streets, but the Jeep splashed through most of them easily. Twice they had to take a detour because a street had been completely flooded.

When they arrived at the La Juliana restaurant, they found the staff already boarding up the windows.

"Yes, we are still open," said a man wearing a poncho and pounding nails out front. "We are just getting ready for the typhoon."

61

"Typhoon?" Callie said. "I thought they called them hurricanes in this hemisphere."

The man nodded. "Sí. The weathermen do. But here on San Esteban the tradition is to call these big storms typhoons. Please, come inside. We are not very busy today, and my cook will be happy for the work."

The La Juliana was a nice place on the fringe of downtown Nuevo Esteban. It had windows on three sides, but one of the sides had already been boarded up, and the staff was working on the second. As the winds hadn't picked up yet, the Hardys and their friends asked for a seat near the remaining unboarded windows.

Based on recommendations from Angela, they ordered local dishes. The cuisine was a mix of Spanish and southwestern cooking. Spicy rice dishes and tortillas were the specialties. The wind howled outside, and the rain pelted the remaining unboarded windows. Lightning lit the sky and thunder echoed off of the nearby mountains. The streets of the small city became progressively more deserted.

"I know this isn't what we had planned for a vacation," Frank said after a loud clap of thunder, "but the weather *is* pretty spectacular."

"You're right," Callie said, "but I'd still rather have sunshine."

Even though it wasn't yet evening, the sky was

very dark by the time they finished their meal.

As they stepped out into the rain and opened their flimsy umbrellas, something across the street caught Joe's eye.

Seeing his troubled look, Iola asked, "What is it, Joe?"

Joe glanced at Frank. Frank nodded grimly.

"We didn't want to mention it before," Joe said, "but that guy has been following us around town."

"Joe and I noticed him hanging around while we were eating," Frank added.

On the other side of the street, about a half block away, a shadowy figure stood in the rain. It looked like a man, though none of them could see his features clearly through the dark shadows.

"I think we should go find out what he wants," Joe said. He handed his umbrella to Iola and splashed across the street toward the lurking stranger. Frank gave his umbrella to Callie and followed Joe.

Before they could reach the mysterious figure, though, the man suddenly turned and dashed into a nearby alley.

7 Chasing Shadows

Joe and Frank took off in hot pursuit of the man.

Driving rain pelted the brothers' bodies as they dashed across the street and into the alley. In moments their clothes were completely soaked through. The wind, warm though it was, triggered goose bumps on their skin.

They spotted the mystery man at the far end of the alley just before he turned the corner. The rain, wind, and thunder made it nearly impossible to hear anything. As they darted out of the adjoining alley a passing flatbed truck nearly ran them over.

The truck honked, and the brothers stopped. Carefully they circled around behind it, and the truck lumbered past.

The Hardys' sneakers quickly filled with water.

They felt as though they were running with lead weights attached to their feet. Their only comfort was that the man they were pursuing faced the same difficulties.

Whoever he was, he knew the streets of Nuevo Esteban better than the brothers did. He ducked into alleys that the Hardys didn't even see.

The third time this happened, they almost lost him. A T intersection dead-ended behind some warehouses, and the culprit was nowhere to be seen. One direction ended in a high wooden fence; the other led to nothing but trees.

Joe pointed to a turned-over trash can near the fence. "Some of that garbage is still dry," he said. "The guy we're following must have knocked it over while running."

Frank nodded, and the two of them sprinted to the dead end. Both brothers were athletic, having spent many hours training for sports at Bayport High. They scrambled over the wooden fence and down the other side with little difficulty.

"There he is!" Frank said. Their quarry splashed through a shin-high puddle in the next street.

The chase led them from the newer parts of the city into the older, more crowded sections of Nuevo Esteban. The alleys they ran through became progressively narrower and were clogged with garbage. The storm had driven most sensible folks indoors, and this worked to the Hardys' advantage; the man they were following was easy to spot on the deserted streets.

The man never stopped running, and not once did he turn back to face them. Because they didn't know the area, the brothers were hard pressed to keep up.

Ten minutes into the chase the suspect disappeared down an alley leading to a four-way intersection. When the Hardys arrived at the crossroads, they found dead ends in all directions. One was a solid brick wall, another a boarded-up factory, and the third a locked door.

Joe looked from one dead end to the other. "Rats!"

Rain sprayed off of Frank's short, dark hair as he whipped his head around, considering their options. He tried the door, but it didn't budge. At the other end of the alley Joe found a loose board in the factory wall.

"Do you think he went in here?" the younger Hardy asked. He peered into the shadowy space beyond. "The roof's leaking something awful, so there are no wet footprints to follow."

Frank's dark eyes strayed to a manhole cover he hadn't noticed before in one street. He shook his head. "Whether he went in there or down the manhole, I'm afraid we've lost him."

The brothers stood for a moment in the rain and wind, and caught their breath.

"Come on," Frank said. "We better get back to the girls."

The route they took back to the restaurant had far fewer twists and turns. Both brothers had studied maps of the city before coming on vacation, so they generally knew how to get back to where they'd started.

Still, it was the better part of twenty minutes before they spotted Callie, Iola, and Angela sitting in the Jeep by the curb outside the restaurant. A police officer stood next to the vehicle. The sight sent a chill up the brothers' spines.

They dashed across the street to the car and the glowering officer. "Are these the boys you were waiting for?" he asked sternly.

"Yes," Callie said.

"Good," the officer replied. "I'll tell our patrols to stop looking for them, then. All of you need to get to shelter. Typhoon Hilary is going to hit this island pretty hard. We don't need any tourists getting swept away." He gave them a grim half smile.

Frank and Joe got into the Jeep. With a nod to the policeman, Callie pulled the vehicle into the rain-swept street. Frank's girlfriend looked relieved. "We were starting to worry," she explained.

"That guy led us on quite a chase," Frank replied. "We ended up down in the old South Village."

"That's a dangerous place," Angela said. "Gangs hang out there."

67

"The streets were pretty deserted," Joe told the girls. "Even gangsters are smart enough to get out of the rain."

"But not my boyfriend, apparently," Iola said.

"So, you lost the guy?" Callie asked.

"Yeah, he disappeared into some alley or something," Frank said.

"Whoever he was," Joe added, "he knew his way around the back streets."

Frank nodded. "I can think of only a couple of people here who might have any reason to follow us," he said. "This guy was about the same size as Jamie Escobar—or Lucas McGill. But neither one of us got a good look at him."

"He seemed too spry to be McGill," Joe said.

"I don't know," Frank replied. "That old guy gets around pretty well. He's popped up suddenly a couple of times and disappeared just as quickly. What do we really know about him, aside from the fact that he claims to be looking out for fellow Americans?"

"Okay, maybe it was him," Joe agreed. "But Escobar's a street kid. He'd know these alleys pretty well."

"It could be just some local mugger," Iola said.

"Why hang around across from the restaurant in the rain, then?" Frank asked.

Callie's brown eyes quickly scanned the drenched group. "Look at us," she said. "We don't look rich enough to be staked out for robbery." She turned her eyes back to the road.

Everyone laughed.

"Angela," Iola said, "do you know anything about McGill or Escobar?"

Iola's cousin furrowed her brow. "Jamie Escobar hangs around the marketplace a lot, flirting with the pretty girls. He's in one of the local gangs, so nobody messes with him."

"What about Lucas McGill?" Joe asked.

"The Gringo?" Angela said. "Everybody in Nuevo Esteban knows him. He's a *very* shady character. He's been picked up by the police many times, but they have never been able to convict him. He's a local black marketeer—has his hands in a lot of small criminal enterprises. If he's following you, you must have something he wants."

"But what?" Iola asked. She looked at Callie and the brothers, and they all shrugged.

"What I'm wondering," Frank said, "is how he got away from us in those dead-end alleys."

"There are a lot of old bootlegger tunnels in the South Village," Angela said. "Smugglers used to operate out of there, too, during the world wars. Volcanic caves run under the whole island. Nobody really knows all the hidden crawl spaces in this old rock. Jorge Tejeda opened some of the tunnels to tourists. You should check them out when the weather clears up."

"*If* it ever clears up," Callie said.

The wind buffeted their Jeep from side to side as they drove, and rain cascading against the windshield made it difficult for Callie to see. They finally found their way to Angela's small second-floor apartment and dropped her off, then headed for their bungalows.

As they drove Iola checked safety information from the hotel brochures. "Our designated emergency shelter is in the basement of Casa Bonita," she said. She looked at the rain outside, which showed no sign of letting up. "Staying in a crowded basement with a bunch of other tourists is *not* my idea of paradise."

"It beats being blown away by a typhoon," Frank noted.

They soon passed over the aging bridge that spanned the river. Rainwater had already swollen the waterway to the edges of its banks, and palm trees swayed dramatically by the sides of the road. Huge waves crashed on the nearby beaches, and clouds of sea spray leaped high into the swirling air.

"Surf's up!" Joe said, smirking.

At Casa Bonita guests were moving their cars behind the hotel, away from the waterfront. The hotel had a good five hundred yards of beach between it and the water at high tide, and a seawall of boulders separated the beach from the hotel. All that sand and rock looked like little protection, though, as the waves grew higher and higher.

"If the hotel sinks, where do we go for shelter?" Callie asked, only half joking.

They left the narrow highway and wound up the even narrower road that led into the hills. Water rushing downhill made driving difficult, but Callie handled it well enough. Fallen trees lay by the roadside as they drove through the junglelike forest. Fortunately none of the logs had blocked the road.

Despite the difficult driving, they soon reached their tiny bungalows. Sheltered by the forest and the height of the cliffs, the small huts seemed to be weathering the storm fairly well.

"Maybe we'd be safer here," Iola said as they pulled up. "The huts have their own electricity supply."

"But the walls are just wood and straw," Frank noted.

"And there are no phones if anything goes wrong," Callie said.

"And one of those big palm trees would make a pretty hefty dent in a bungalow roof," Joe added.

"Okay," Iola said. "I get the point. We'll stick to the official emergency plan."

"You know what they say: When in San Esteban . . . ," Frank said, smiling at Iola.

They scurried through the rain into their respective huts, trying not to get any wetter than they already were.

"You think it's worth changing into dry clothes?" Joe asked as he stripped off his shirt and wrung it out in the tub. "We'll probably just get soaked again."

"Callie and I each packed some travel ponchos," Frank said. "We hoped we wouldn't need them, but now seems like a good time to break them out, huh?"

Joe smiled. "I'm glad my brother and his girlfriend think ahead," he said. "Iola and I planned only for sun and surf." He stripped off the rest of his clothes, wrung them out, and put them in a plastic laundry bag. He quickly changed into a new shirt and shorts. Frank found the ponchos and then changed as well. They threw their other clothes in their duffel bags and opened the pouches that contained the bright orange rain ponchos.

As the brothers unfolded the slickers, a huge crack of thunder shook the tiny building. The brothers froze in midaction as the sound died away.

"That was close by," Frank said.

"Too close," Joe agreed. A moment later he sniffed the air. "Do you smell smoke?" he asked.

Frank looked around the small room. An orange light near the rear corner caught his eye. "Fire!"

8 The Storm Breaks

Joe grabbed the blanket off his bed and ran to the corner. He beat the blanket against the flames but couldn't smother them. "Lightning must have hit the hut," he said.

"Maybe," Frank replied. He quickly retrieved the fire extinguisher from beside the hut's tiny electric heater. He popped off the safety lock, pointed the nozzle toward the base of the flames, and pulled the trigger.

The extinguisher hissed, a small cloud puffed out of the nozzle, and a tiny stream of bubbly liquid leaked onto the floor. Frank looked at the date stamped on the side of the canister. "Expired!" he said, tossing the useless extinguisher aside.

"Soak one of the sheets with water," Joe suggested,

still beating at the fire with his blanket.

"In the tub, or outside?" Frank asked wryly as he yanked the covers off his bed and dashed into the bathroom. In just moments he returned with the sheet thoroughly soaked, and joined Joe in trying to extinguish the flames.

Sweat poured down their faces as they battled the blaze. Despite their efforts, the fire climbed up the hut's grass wall toward the ceiling. "It's no use," Joe said.

"Get your stuff and head outside," Frank said. "If the extinguisher in the girls' cabin works, we may still have a chance."

Both brothers dropped their makeshift fire blankets and grabbed their duffel bags and ponchos from beside the door. As they stepped outside Iola ran up to them, holding her orange poncho in one hand.

"Help!" she cried. "Fire!"

The Hardys dropped their gear and ran to the other hut. They found the girls' bags lying outside and Callie standing beside the hut. She was aiming a sputtering fire extinguisher toward a strip of burning thatch near the door.

"This thing doesn't work!" she said angrily.

"Ours is no good either," Frank said.

"And our hut is on fire too," Joe added.

Callie looked around, panic in her face. "What?"

she asked, not believing him. "Are you all right?"

"We're fine," Frank replied. "Got our gear out too—same as you."

"I think lightning struck the huts," Callie said. "We heard a huge bang just before the fire broke out."

"If only the cabins had phones!" Iola said, moaning.

"And our cell phones don't work either," Joe said angrily.

"We'll have to drive out of the jungle and get help," Frank said. He pulled his poncho on over his head, even though he was already soaked and sweaty. The others did the same as they headed for the Jeep.

When they reached the battered old vehicle, though, they immediately noticed that it looked lopsided.

"Did it sink into the mud?" Callie asked. The entire road leading downhill looked like a mud slide.

"No," Frank said, stooping beside the Jeep. "The tires are flat."

"All of them?" Joe asked.

"Just the two right tires," Frank said, examining the flats.

"Could the lightning have blown out the tires *and* set the huts on fire?" Iola asked.

"On a one-in-a-million shot, maybe," Joe said.

"I think there's a more likely explanation," Frank said as rain dripped off his orange hood. "Someone did this on purpose."

"The same person who was following us earlier today?" Callie asked.

"Could be," Joe said. "Either someone's out to get us, or someone on this island doesn't like tourists in general."

"But why?" Iola asked.

"If we knew the answer to that," Frank said, "we'd know who was causing this trouble."

"I don't see any tracks," Joe said, looking around the small clearing. "But rain could have washed them away." He peered into the jungle and down the road but didn't see anyone.

"There's nothing we can do about the cabins, then," Callie said. "There goes our vacation—up in smoke."

For a moment none of them said anything. They stood beside the Jeep and watched the fires consume their vacation bungalows. The poncho-clad teens looked like four orange ghosts in the twilight.

"Come on," Frank finally said. "Maybe if we meet someone on the road we can still get the authorities up here to save at least a bit of these bungalows."

"What about our bags?" Callie asked.

"We'll leave them in the Jeep," Joe said. "It's not going anywhere, and the hike will be easier if we travel light."

They stashed their gear in the Jeep and dug a flashlight and some flares out of the glove compartment. Frank locked the car and stashed the keys inside the fuel door, which he left ajar. "No sense losing the keys on our trek downhill," he said. "And it's not like anyone's going to steal a car with two flat tires."

"Do you think the walk to the hotel will be difficult?" Callie asked.

"Let's just say that I wouldn't be surprised if we did as much sliding as walking," Frank said, looking at the muddy road. "Let's get going before the storm gets any worse."

They stuck to the edges of the road. The rain had already turned the center of it into a narrow, rapid stream of mud. Sometimes they walked on one side, sometimes the other, always choosing the less hazardous course. They crossed over the muddy road using the few stepping stones that were in the road.

"How far is it to the hotel?" Iola asked.

"At least five miles," Joe replied.

"Five miles didn't seem so far in the bright sunshine," Callie said. Even with their ponchos, all of them were getting very wet.

Rain cascaded through the dense forest canopy. The raindrops sounded like nails falling on the leaves. Wind shook the upper branches, and many of the trees swayed in the strong wind.

"Next time remind me to vacation in the desert,"

Iola said, looking drenched and miserable.

Shadows moved through the trees on either side of the road. The teens couldn't tell whether the moving shapes were animals or just branches blowing in the wind. In the distance they heard the low wail of Nuevo Esteban's storm sirens, warning people to take shelter.

"Being caught outside when this typhoon hits is *not* my idea of fun," Joe said.

"Staying in a burning hut didn't seem like a better option, but I'm open to suggestions," Frank replied.

"I suggest we keep moving," Callie said. "It's not going to get better if we stand around talking." She bravely trudged forward through the rain and the darkness.

"We could always go back to the car and wait for help," Iola said. "I'm sure the Jeep's engine still works, and we could use the heaters to dry off. They must have a list of guests who are supposed to use the shelter at the hotel. Someone's bound to come looking for us."

"If they're able," Frank said. "I doubt people will be moving around much when the storm gets worse—no matter who's missing."

"They'll probably have so many folks in that shelter, and they'll be so busy, they won't even notice we're gone," Joe said.

"Besides," Frank continued, "the typhoon will

toss that car around like a toy. You've seen pictures of ships stranded miles inland by hurricanes. We wouldn't be any safer there than we are here."

"Maybe not," Iola said, shivering, "but we'd be warmer and drier." She let out a long, exasperated sigh, then followed Callie's lead.

The wind and rain and the condition of the road all grew worse as the four teens made their way downhill. The noise surrounding them became almost deafening; it was a mixture of howling wind, driving rain, rustling leaves, and creaking tree trunks. The deteriorating path forced them to move through the jungle along the side of the road.

"Did you see that?" Callie called, stopping and peering into the brush.

"See what?" Frank asked. They had to yell over the din.

"There's something moving in the jungle to the right," she replied.

"It's probably just some animal trying to get out of the storm," Joe suggested.

"Ha! I hope it has better luck than we're having," Iola quipped.

Something whizzed across the path ahead of them, moving so quickly that they could hardly see it. They heard the brush move as the thing zipped through to the road. A corner of one leaf fluttered toward the ground before being whipped away by the wind.

"What was *that*?" Iola asked.

"A bird or bat, maybe?" Joe suggested.

"It was moving awfully fast," Callie said.

"Hurricane winds can drive a piece of straw through an oak tree," Frank noted.

"And that's supposed to make us feel better?" Iola asked.

"Ouch!" yelped Callie.

"What's wrong?" Frank, Joe, and Iola asked simultaneously.

"Something pricked me in the leg," Callie replied. "I think I've got a thorn caught in my poncho or something. Hang on while I try to get it out." She stopped, and started pulling on the folds of the bright orange poncho.

She crinkled her nose. "That's funny," she said.

"What?" Frank asked.

"It's a long thorn attached to a berry or something. But the berry kind of looks like a bright green bead."

They all looked to where she was pointing.

In the hem of Callie's poncho they saw a slender, needlelike object. A bright plastic bead about the size of a marble was stuck to one end.

Frank's eyes narrowed. "That's no thorn. It's a blowgun dart!"

9 Into the Typhoon

"Get down!" Frank said. "Use the trees for cover."

The teens crowded as close to a nearby large palm tree trunk as they could and crouched down. The Hardys scanned the woods but saw only trees and wind-tossed foliage.

"Where do you think the dart came from?" Callie asked fearfully.

"Are you sure it's a dart?" Iola asked, fighting to remain calm. "The bead thing looks like it could be a berry. I thought blowgun darts had feathers on them."

"Not modern blowgun darts," Joe replied. "The bead is attached to a long needle that's fitted into the blowgun's barrel. The sphere gives extra oomph to the missile when it's fired. The tube works almost like a rifle barrel—"

"We can explain how it works later," Frank said, cutting his brother off. His gaze flitted back and forth across the flooded road. "Right now we need to find out who shot at us, locate where he is, and deal with him before he can hurt anyone."

"D-Do you think the dart is *poisoned*?" Callie asked, looking at a scratch on her calf.

"There's no way to tell," Frank replied. He put his arm around her shoulder and pulled the dart from the hem of her poncho. "Do you feel okay?"

"I think so."

"Don't worry about it, then." He stuck a small piece of bark onto the point of the needle and put the dart into his breast pocket. "Let us know if you start feeling funny."

"Easy for you to say, Frank Hardy," Callie replied. Under her bright orange poncho she was as white as a sheet.

Just then something whipped by them. A green-tailed dart appeared in the tree trunk above their heads.

"Move now—while he reloads!" Joe said. He headed into the brush behind the tree. Frank and the rest followed.

"I thought you wanted to find him," Iola said.

"That'd be nice," Joe replied, "but I'd rather he didn't find us."

They ran through the rain forest, pushing the dense overgrowth out of the way. The darkness and rain made seeing and hearing difficult. Several times something whizzed through the leaves on either side of them or over their heads. The teens couldn't be sure if the faint noise came from the passage of some flying creature, falling debris, or a blowgun dart—but they assumed the worst. Fortunately no one was hit.

"With this wind, and the rain coming down, whoever is shooting can't be very accurate," Frank said.

"The foliage works to our advantage too," Joe added. "We should keep moving—not give him any easy targets." He pushed ahead through the thick green undergrowth.

They kept moving as fast as they could, darting around the brush and fallen trees as the thunder echoed in their ears. Within a few minutes they came to a dense patch of undergrowth and had to slow down a bit and work their way through. Joe took the lead, bulldozing ahead like a first-string running back breaking through the line. Frank and the girls followed close behind.

"How's your leg?" Frank asked Callie.

"Fine, I think," she said. "It's not stinging or anything."

"That's a good sign," Joe called back. "Maybe whoever's doing this is only trying to scare us."

"Well, he's doing a good job," Iola commented.

"I'll take a closer look at the dart once we shake this guy," Frank said. "I'm sure you'll be okay."

Callie nodded bravely, but her lower lip trembled.

Something whizzed over their heads as Joe finally got through the tangled undergrowth. Up ahead the jungle thinned out. They all broke into a sprint once again.

"These orange ponchos are making us easy targets," Iola said, glancing over her shoulder as she ran.

"But we're hard to hit," Joe noted. "The sniper can't pick out our bodies under the billowing plastic."

A peal of thunder shook the ground. A huge tree split in half and fell toward the teens.

"Look out!" Frank called, pushing Callie out of the way. Joe and Iola dived aside as the tree crashed down next to them. Frank grunted in pain.

"Are you all right?" Callie asked.

"I'm not hurt bad," the elder Hardy said, "but I'm trapped. I can't move."

Joe knelt down and examined his brother. "His feet are pinned under the log," he said to the girls. "Help me lift it? Frank, when we lift, try to crawl out."

Frank gritted his teeth and nodded. Joe, Iola, and Callie wrapped their arms around the palm tree's soggy bark and heaved with all their might. The fallen tree inched up slightly, and Frank crawled out from underneath.

"Can you walk?" Joe asked.

"I think so," Frank said, gingerly testing his weight on his feet.

Joe looped an arm under his older brother's armpit; Callie did the same on the other side. "Lean on us for a while," she said.

Frank nodded and winced slightly.

Iola took the lead, and they forged ahead again.

They moved more slowly as Frank tried to regain his footing. Iola glanced back frequently, checking on her companions and looking for the blowgun sniper.

The storm showed no signs of stopping. The wind continued to howl, and the rain pelted through the dense leaves overhead. Their footing grew progressively less solid as the soil under their feet turned entirely to slippery mud.

A few scared animals crossed their path as the friends trudged onward. A wild boar ran past, heading toward the island's interior. Shortly after that a large, iguana-like lizard fell out of a splintered tree, nearly landing on the girls' heads. It, too, scrambled off into the brush.

A fallen log in the road soon blocked their progress. Callie and Iola stooped to move it out of their way while Joe supported Frank. As they lifted the log, three giant centipedes scuttled out from beneath. The girls jumped, but the insects seemed more intent on escaping than causing trouble. The bugs quickly disappeared into the undergrowth, and the girls sighed in relief.

The teens kept moving as quickly as they could. Frank soon shook off the effects of being pinned under the tree. His ankles ached, but he managed to keep up with the rest. Helping Frank walk had tired out Joe and Callie, and now they moved more slowly than any of them would have liked.

Occasionally the leaves around them would ripple with some unseen force—perhaps another blowgun dart zipping past, though it could just as easily have been the driving rain, or debris whipped up by the wind. The harrowing journey began to take its toll on the teens' nerves as well as their bodies.

"We have to stop soon," Iola said, gasping.

"Just a little farther," Joe said.

"How are we going to find our way back to the hotel?" Callie asked.

"We'll figure that out once we're sure we've lost this sniper," Frank replied. "Keep moving. I think I see some light up ahead. It may be a clearing."

"Maybe we can use it to get our bearings," Joe suggested.

He and the others ran as quickly as they could in the direction Frank indicated. The wind tugged at their ponchos, and the rain stung their exposed skin. Water seeped up their sleeves and down their necks, further soaking their clothing. Their feet felt like blocks of lead.

Spattered with mud and drenched to the bone, the four finally emerged from the jungle. What Frank had seen was not actually a clearing within the forest, but a bare spot on top of a seaside bluff. A hundred feet below on either side stretched the Caribbean, its waters whipped into a white-capped frenzy by the approaching hurricane.

Joe bent over and put his hands on his knees to catch his breath. He scanned the forest behind them. "I think," he said, panting, "that we may have lost . . . the sniper."

"I sure . . . hope so," Iola replied, also gasping for air. "It looks like . . . we're out of room to run." She cast a wary eye over the bluff to the raging sea far below.

"Which is the way . . . back to Nuevo Esteban?" Callie asked.

Frank looked north and south along the coast. The land curved away in either direction, and he saw no sign of the city through the storm. "It has to be to the left," he said.

Joe nodded his agreement. "Let's rest a minute," he suggested.

"Just for a minute," Callie said, shivering. "We need to get out of this storm."

Exhausted, they all flopped down into the mud on top of the bluff. While Joe and Iola kept a careful watch on the forest, Frank pulled the bark-capped blowgun dart out of his pocket. He held it up, hoping to catch any last rays of sunlight that managed to leak from beneath the black storm clouds.

"I don't see any discoloration on the needle," he said, squinting and examining the dart carefully. He ran his fingers over the slender metal shaft and then held his fingertips to his nose.

Callie looked at him apprehensively. Her pale hand shook as she brushed her drenched blond hair back out of her eyes.

"I don't smell anything either," Frank concluded.

"What's that mean?" Iola asked. Dark circles ringed her gray eyes, and her skin looked as ashen as Callie's.

"It means the dart's probably not poisoned," Joe said.

Callie heaved a deep sigh of relief. "Thank goodness," she said.

"Nonpoisonous darts can give you a nasty sting," Frank said, "or even kill if they hit you in the right spot."

"My brother the optimist," Joe said.

Frank laughed and gave Callie a quick hug. "You're not poisoned, but we're still in a bind here," he said. He and Joe looked and felt as beat as the girls. They needed a safe place to rest and recover—and they needed to find it soon. Sitting in the wind and rain wasn't doing them any good.

Out to sea they saw the full fury of the hurricane

building. The waves towered like blue gray mountains, their white peaks whipping into blurs of spray. Thunder crashed, and lightning lit the dark sky. The whole world seemed bathed in eerie green light—the kind of illumination that foretells the coming of a terrible storm.

Joe stood. "We need to get out of here."

He gave Iola a hand to her feet, and Frank and Callie helped each other up. As they rose a strange, rumbling burble built up around them. Suddenly the top of the bluff gave way—and all four teens plunged down the cliff face toward the raging sea.

10 Storm Tide Rising

The mud slide surged around the teens, causing Iola and Callie to scream.

"Try to grab on to something!" Frank shouted.

"Like what?" Joe called back. "The whole hillside's given way!"

The Hardys and their girlfriends scrambled through the mud, trying to get a grip on anything that might stop their slide.

"It's no use!" Iola cried.

Frank shot his arm out and grabbed a bush at the slide's edge. The branches were thorny and cut the skin on Frank's palm, but the plant held. Callie caught hold of his belt and held on tight. "Iola! Joe!" she called.

But they were too far away to grab on. Joe and

his girlfriend tumbled down the muddy slope toward the rock-lined shore. Joe seized Iola in his arms. "Hang tight," he said. She nodded and wrapped her arms tightly around his waist.

Joe rolled sideways, against the flow of the slide. Rocks and earth battered their bodies. Rain and floodwaters washed over them, threatening to drown them even before the rocks below could shatter their bones.

Suddenly they hit something hard and stopped sliding.

"Joe! Iola! Are you all right?" Frank shouted down from above.

The younger Hardy and his girlfriend wiped the mud off their faces and opened their eyes. They were lying on top of a small, brush-covered ledge near the base of the bluff. The remnants of the mud slide gurgled past them, less than an arm's length away.

"We are *so* lucky," Iola said quietly.

"Lucky?" Joe said. "What do you think I was aiming for with all that rolling?" He smiled at her and then called up to Frank and Callie, "We're okay!"

"I don't think we can climb back up!" Iola said, shouting to make herself heard above the storm.

"Stay there!" Frank replied. "We'll make our way down to you."

He and Callie took a few moments to plot the safest course down the bluff's face, then carefully made their way down to their friends.

The bushy ledge Joe and Iola had landed on lay less than a dozen yards from the rocky shore. Sea mist, tossed up from the tall waves, filled the air. The shore was even wetter, it seemed, than the jungle had been.

"It's a miracle that none of us were hurt," Frank said, looking back the way they'd come.

"One thing's for sure," Joe said. "That blowgun sniper will have trouble following us now."

"If he has any sense," Iola said, "he's somewhere safe and dry by now."

"I wish I could say the same for us," Callie added. Her brown eyes reflected a flash of lightning.

"We'll head south along the coast," Frank said. "We know the town's in that direction."

"I'm pretty sure that most of this coastline is made of cliffs," Iola said.

"Maybe," Joe said. "But maybe there'll be a place we can climb up. We better get moving, though. This storm is moving in very fast."

They fought their way along the coast. The wind attempted to pound them into the cliff face, the rain tried to beat them into the ground, and the rising waves threatened to drag them out to sea. Though the air temperature remained hot, the rain and wind had sucked most of the warmth out of the teenagers' bodies.

The rocky shore provided no shelter, and the cliff face didn't allow a climb back up to the jungle. All four of them felt miserable. There was nothing to do, though, but press on.

The sound of the storm around them was incredible. The wind, rain, and surf built into a cacophony that made their heads throb. With chaos swirling all around, it became increasingly difficult to concentrate.

More than once they almost lost their footing on the rocks. Joe cut his shin on a sharp boulder. They stopped just long enough for him to tear a makeshift bandage from his T-shirt.

"I hope there are no land sharks around to be drawn by the scent of blood," he joked.

"With the way this storm is coming in," Frank replied, "I'd be just as worried about *regular* sharks if I were you."

They all laughed, though their situation wasn't at all funny. They soon realized that if they didn't find shelter before the worst of the storm hit, they were goners. As soon as Joe tied off his bandage, they got moving again.

All four of them had studied maps of San Esteban, and they knew they couldn't be very far up the coast from either their rented cottages—at least what was left of them—or Casa Bonita. Yet as they looked south along the shore they saw no sign of their destination. They all felt disheartened, but no one mentioned it.

Suddenly a rogue wave, taller than a two-story

building, surged out of the sea and crashed into the teens. It smashed them to the ground, and the backwash threatened to pull them into the raging surf. Joe, Iola, and Frank crouched down and grabbed on to nearby boulders, but Callie lost her footing.

"Help!" she cried as she was dragged into the ocean.

Both Frank and Joe tried to grab her. Frank missed, but Joe twined his fingers around Callie's outstretched hand and hung on tight. Iola anchored her feet under one of the boulders and grabbed on to both Hardys' belts. Frank grabbed Callie's other hand.

For an endless moment they hung there, trapped in a deadly tug-of-war with the sea for possession of their friend. Finally the surf subsided, and Callie climbed back over the rocks to her companions.

She was battered, bruised, and even more soaked than before, but otherwise little the worse for her terrifying experience. Frank gave her a hug, and they all continued up the rocky slope, farther away from the perilous waves.

Moving on the higher rocks slowed their journey considerably. Plus what was left of the last dull gray light was rapidly waning, and they still couldn't make out the lights of Nuevo Esteban or their hotel.

"Maybe the power's been knocked out," suggested Joe.

"It wouldn't surprise me," Frank replied.

"I'd be surprised if it hadn't been, with this weather," Iola added.

They didn't want to use the flashlight they'd rescued from the Jeep any sooner than necessary, but now it seemed they might need it to avoid a perilous misstep along the rocky shore.

Just then Frank's sharp eyes spotted a dark blot on the dim gray cliff face. "It might be a cave," he said. "There are supposed to be caves along this shore."

"Let's hope so," Iola said. "We could use a break from the wind and rain."

"And the waves," added Callie.

They made their way toward the dark shape as quickly as they could and reached it just as night fell. Sure enough it was a wide cave that stretched back into the cliff.

"I don't see the end of it," Joe said, peering inside. "It'll be a good place for us to dry off for a moment and catch our breath."

"Sounds good," Frank said. They cautiously moved inside.

The cave mouth was about thirteen feet tall, and wide enough so that all four of them could walk side by side. The floor and walls were smooth and slick with mist from the pounding surf. The tunnel led deep into the cliff, up away from the shore.

Venturing a short distance inside, they quickly

found relief from the rain, wind, and surf. The passage narrowed until the roof hung just over their heads, and they had to walk two by two.

The cave wound through the cliff face with no clear direction or purpose. Callie had a solar-charged penlight attached to a key chain on her belt. It didn't give off enough light to be much use outdoors, but in the confined passage it proved sufficient. They decided to use its dim light to navigate, and save their flashlight for later.

They walked up the tunnel until it was dry, then took turns looking the other way while each wrung out his or her wet clothing.

"Too bad we don't have anything to build a fire with," Joe said. "This place would be pretty comfortable with a campfire going."

"Let's not move in just yet," Frank said. "As soon as we've rested, we should try to get back to town."

"I'm not looking forward to going out in that storm again," said Iola.

"Maybe we won't have to," Callie said, brightening. "Remember the story Angela told us about old bootlegger caves running under the island and city? Maybe this is one of them. Maybe we could follow it back to town."

"It'd have to be a really long cave," Joe noted.

"It's worth looking into," Frank said. He stood and started hiking farther away from the cave entrance. The others followed.

They walked on an uphill slope for about ten minutes before the tunnel angled down once more. "Hang on," Joe said, stopping. "Listen."

They all stood quietly.

"I hear water," Iola said.

"Yeah," Joe replied. "That's what I thought. It's just leading us to the ocean again."

"Let's go back the way we came," Frank said. "Following this tunnel when we don't know where it comes out is probably riskier than hiking along the coast again. Maybe we can find a way up the cliff that we didn't spot before."

They all agreed and headed back toward the cave entrance. They quickly reached the tunnel's high point and began angling toward the rocky beach once more.

A few moments later, though, a shocking sight greeted their eyes.

"The tunnel," Callie said, gasping. "It's filled with water!"

11 Storm Surge

Frank hauled out the flashlight and turned it on to get a better look. Sure enough, water had completely filled the passage in front of the teens.

"But it was clear just a few minutes ago!" Iola said.

"The rising tide and the storm surge must have filled it up quickly," Joe said. He shook his head angrily. "We should have been more careful!"

"There was no way we could have known," Frank said. "Come on. Maybe the other end of the tunnel is still clear."

"But we heard water at that end," Callie said.

"It might come out into a different cove," Frank said. "Storm surges are funny things; they can affect one bay and not the next. It all depends on the shape of the island and which direction the storm is coming from."

"I guess we can give it a try," Iola said.

"We have no choice," Joe added. "If we're trapped, we'll just have to hope we've got enough air in here to last out the storm."

"And hope the tide doesn't rise any higher," Callie said.

"No sense worrying about it until we've checked the other end of the tunnel," Frank said. He turned off the flashlight, and they all trekked up the passage by the dim glow of Callie's penlight.

They quickly reached the downward slope they'd found earlier. They kept going until they heard sloshing water once more. Shortly after that they saw water on the tunnel floor. Frank went forward and tasted it. "Seawater," he said. "I'd hoped it might be an underground spring."

"That means the cave connects to the ocean again," Callie said.

Frank flicked on their flashlight and shone it ahead of the group. "The tunnel looks like it opens up ahead," he said. "Wait here while I take a look. There's no sense in all of us getting wet again if we don't have to."

He climbed down the tunnel and waded into the brine. The cold water made Frank shiver. He held the flashlight above his head and out of the water as the liquid rose up to his waist.

Before him lay a large cavern filled with foamy saltwater. Oddly enough, a speedboat with a broken rope hanging off the prow floated in the middle of the strange underground lake. Frank saw no entrance in the cave big enough to admit the craft.

"You won't believe what's down here," he called back to the others. "You know that stolen speedboat from yesterday? Well, we found it."

"Beth Becker's boat?" Iola asked.

"Yeah. There's a big cave down here, and the boat's floating in it."

"Should we come down?" Joe called to him.

"Hang on a moment," Frank said. He shone the light carefully around the cave's perimeter until he found what he was looking for. "Yes!" he called. "The cave is pretty full of water, but there's an exit on the far side."

Joe, Iola, and Callie splashed into the cave behind Frank.

"*Brr!* This water is cold!" Iola said.

"How did the stolen boat get in here?" Callie asked.

"There must be a seaward exit when the tide isn't so high," Joe said. "After they stole it, the pirates must have stashed the boat here."

"Too bad we can't drive the boat back to the hotel," Iola said.

"With the sea so rough, we'd never make it," Frank said. "The boat *is* a good sign, though."

"How so?" Callie asked.

"Whoever stashed it here must have had a way out," Joe said. "Maybe they went out the way they came in . . . but if this actually is an old bootlegger tunnel, they probably had another way out too. A dry-land exit."

"On top of the cliff, you mean," Iola said. "Well, what are we waiting for? Let's go!"

"Keep toward the edge of the pool and walk carefully," Frank cautioned. "We don't know how deep this water is."

They moved quickly, but cautiously, across the open span of water to the cave exit. They stumbled a few times, but no one vanished into the brine. As they crossed the flooded cavern the water level kept rising. Frank's initial observation proved correct: The new passage did lead up and out of the cave.

"I'm just really hoping this tunnel leads out to the cliff," Joe said. He took the big flashlight from Frank and led the way.

They hiked until they were out of the water again, then switched back to Callie's penlight to conserve their flashlight's batteries. They also paused briefly to wring out their clothes again.

"I thought that a vacation meant taking a break from doing the wash!" Iola said, managing a smirk.

The water continued to rise quickly behind them, and it soon filled to the level of the cave's roof.

"There's no turning back now," Callie said.

"For the water to rush in like that, the air has to be escaping from these caves somehow," Joe said. "This tunnel seems to be the only possible way."

"And the only way to find out is for us to keep going," Frank noted.

Callie took the lead, to give Frank's bruised ankles and Joe's wounded shin a break.

They traveled up the winding tunnel until they could no longer hear the water rushing in behind them. The fact that they hadn't run out of tunnel yet made them feel better, though this was mitigated somewhat by the fact that no end to the cave was in sight.

Exhausted, they finally decided to take a brief rest on a dry, flat stretch of the passage. They turned off their lights to conserve the batteries, and took turns keeping watch while the others slept.

They couldn't be sure how long they'd slept, but they woke feeling slightly refreshed—though very cold.

"I don't hear any water behind us," Frank said as they got ready to hike again.

"And we haven't run out of air yet," Joe added. "That's a good sign."

"And I think we have *definitely* lost that sniper by now," Callie said. The rest of them chuckled.

They walked among the dark shadows for a long time, seeing no light nor a way out. Callie's penlight finally gave out, and they switched over to the flashlight they'd taken from the Jeep.

They conserved the light when they could, turning it off when they were resting, or when the way ahead seemed straight and hazard free. Finally they came to a place where the passageway split in two.

"Too bad the bootleggers didn't leave any signs telling us which way led to town," Iola commented.

"The bootleggers knew the way," Frank said, "and wanted to make sure that anyone following them *didn't*."

"Have you noticed that both of these new passages are wet?" Joe asked.

"Yeah," Frank replied.

"Does that mean that we're headed down again and didn't notice it?" Callie asked.

"I don't think so," Frank said. "The walls and ceiling are damp too. I think the water's seeping down from the surface somehow." He held his hand under a drop, caught it, and put it to his tongue. "It's freshwater."

"That's a good sign, isn't it?" Iola asked. "We must be getting closer to a way out."

"It could just be filtering through the rock," Frank noted.

"Always the optimist!" Callie said, clearly frustrated. She gave him a playful punch in the shoulder.

"Hey, Frank—the walls of this passage aren't

damp," Joe said, indicating the left-hand tunnel, "only the floor is." He smiled. "I think the water is trickling in from the right-hand passage."

"Good thinking, Joe," Frank replied. "That makes the right-hand passage our best bet. The water needs to enter—and we need to exit."

"Let's go," Iola said.

"Even being in a typhoon sounds good after being underground for so long," Callie commented.

They trudged up the damp passage. It seemed to start steadily upward, but it was no straighter than any of the other paths they'd traversed. As they walked their flashlight began to dim.

"I don't want to be trapped down here in total darkness," Iola complained.

"Good news, then," Joe said. "I think I see a light ahead."

"There's more water running down the tunnel floor, too," Frank noted. "We must be getting close to the surface."

Fifteen minutes later they reached a makeshift wooden door that covered the cave entrance. Cracks between the boards let weak daylight filter in from outside. A small but steady stream of water seeped under the door.

"The good news," Joe said, peering through the cracks, "is that we've found a way out."

"What's the bad news?" Iola asked.

"I think the storm has gotten worse."

"We must have been in the tunnels all night long," Frank said, stepping up beside Joe. "It's hard to tell with the storm, but I think it's morning."

They all could hear the sound of the typhoon raging outside. Joe opened the door and looked around. "The door is in an alcove at the side of the cave," he said. "It's kind of protected from the wind and the rain."

"Maybe we should just stay here, then," Callie said. "It seems safe enough."

As she spoke the ground shook, and a cascade of rocks tumbled down from above the cave entrance.

"Only if being buried alive is your idea of fun," Iola replied.

"Iola's right," Joe said. "The hurricane is making the cave entrance unstable."

"There may be people out looking for us too," Frank said. "We don't want them wasting their time, or getting hurt on our account."

Callie frowned. "You're right," she said. "I just hate to see any of *us* getting hurt either."

"We'll be careful," Frank said, giving her a reassuring hug.

"As careful as anyone can be, roaming into a typhoon," Joe added with a wink.

They adjusted their ponchos, made what few preparations they could, and turned toward the entrance. Another batch of rocks tumbled past the cave mouth just before they stepped out. They hung back inside until the stones stopped falling, then quickly sprinted into the jungle.

The cave was part of a hillside and overlooked the ocean. Though it hardly seemed possible, the storm had grown worse since they first entered the tunnels. The sea was a sheet of white-capped waves. Thunder shook the hills with frightening regularity, and the rain fell in massive sheets.

"I think I see the hotel!" Joe called, shouting to be heard over the wind. He pointed to a white-and-green shape that loomed behind the storm-battered trees downhill.

"Thank goodness," said Callie.

"It looks like we've come out somewhere below our cabins," Frank said. "Come on, let's go."

Stumbling downhill through the drenched forest, they quickly found the trail that led from their cabins. This lower stretch wasn't as washed out as the part they had traveled the previous day, so their journey became somewhat easier.

They climbed over downed trees and dodged falling branches and other debris. The wind and the rain made the trek difficult, but, nonetheless, they were all happy to be out in the open air once more.

Hope filled their hearts as they rounded the final bend of the road before the hotel. They began to sprint, knowing that safety was—at last—in sight.

Near Casa Bonita they suddenly stopped dead.

Rain lashed the hotel's white-painted sides, and downed power lines writhed around its perimeter. Huge waves splashed over the beach seawall, threatening the hotel lobby. Black smoke leaked from the building's upper floors.

Despite the wind and rain and surf, Casa Bonita was on fire.

12 No Shelter

For a moment, the four teens stood in stunned silence. Between the wind, the rain, the fire, and the sparking power lines, Casa Bonita—their shelter from the storm—had become a disaster area.

Hotel patrons and staff were milling around outside, trying to cope with the catastrophe. Rain and wind lashed the people, forcing many of them to crouch at times. The broken power lines threatened to electrocute anyone who got too close.

Suddenly a balcony on one of the upper floors collapsed. It crashed into the parking lot six stories below and shattered into a million pieces. Fortunately no one had been standing on it or under it, and no one was hurt.

"Come on," Joe said. "Let's see what we can do to help."

The four teens sprinted through the rain and wind toward the beleaguered hotel.

"I think we were better off in the cave!" Iola said.

"We may end up *living* in that cave before all this is over," Callie replied.

"If the hurricane doesn't flatten this whole place," Joe said, "maybe we can figure out who's causing the rest of the trouble—the darts, the bull, the creatures in our bungalows . . ."

The hotel's problems escalated in the few seconds it took the Hardys and their girlfriends to get to the front entrance. They found Renee Aranya milling around in the confused crowd. She seemed uncertain what to do.

"Where are the fire and emergency vehicles?" Frank asked her.

"All the phone and power lines are down," she said. "They don't even know we're in trouble."

"Are all the patrons out of the hotel?" Joe asked.

"I think so, yes," she said. "You four were the only ones missing."

"I hate to be the bearer of more bad news," Joe said, "but our bungalows were destroyed by fires and the storm."

"And the road's washed out," Iola added. "That's why it took us all night to get here."

Aranya nodded slowly. She looked shell shocked. "We knew about the road. We sent people to look for you, but the storm got to be too much. And now . . . *this!*" Her tear-filled eyes strayed to the smoke pouring from the building's upper floors.

"Did you send someone into town for the fire department?" Callie asked.

"Yes, but they haven't come back yet," Aranya replied. "The guests who had their own cars have left as well."

"We can't wait for rescue," Frank said. "We need to get everyone out of here immediately. It's too dangerous to stay."

Renee Aranya nodded slowly. Her eyes grew steely and determined, and she wiped the tears from her cheeks.

"How many vehicles do you have?" Joe asked.

"The shuttle bus and two vans," Aranya said.

Frank nodded. "How many injured people are there?"

"Just a handful."

"Good. Put them all into one van," Frank said. "We'll help the rest of the hotel guests get into the bus. Then we can follow in the last car."

Aranya nodded. "You must have some emergency training."

"We've been in our share of tough situations," Joe admitted.

Aranya organized her staff. Soon all of the injured

guests were loaded aboard the first van. The Hardys and their girlfriends helped the other guests into the repainted school bus. The shuttle was nearly full by the time the first van pulled away.

The hotel continued to burn, though the heavy rains seemed to slow the fire a bit. Downed power lines, sparking and hissing like snakes, continued to writhe across the parking lot.

Renee Aranya took one last, long look at the hotel as the bus pulled out of the parking lot. "It was my dream," she said mournfully.

"I think everyone's safe," Callie said. "We should get out of here ourselves."

"Hold up!" someone called.

They turned and saw Lucas McGill walking toward them. The Gringo was supporting a groggy and wet Beth Becker. "You almost missed the last two," he said.

Joe went and helped the older man with Ms. Becker. "Is she all right?" Joe asked.

"She said something fell on her," The Gringo replied. "But she ain't bleeding, and I don't think she has a concussion."

"I *hate* this vacation," Ms. Becker said, moaning.

"Get her in the van," Frank said, turning to the others. "Climb in, everyone. I'll drive." He hopped into the driver's seat, found the keys already in the ignition, and started the vehicle. Iola and Renee Aranya helped The Gringo and Joe load Beth Becker into the back. Callie swung into the passenger seat.

"We're in," said Joe. "Let's go before the storm gets any worse."

Frank pulled the van out of the six-inch-deep puddle that had once been the hotel parking lot, and onto the highway. The road was hardly dry, and he had to fight the current to keep from running off the side. "I wish we had that Jeep right now," he said.

"Don't tell me something happened to the Jeep, too!" Renee Aranya cried, moaning.

"A couple of tires blew at the same time the cabins caught fire," Joe said, glossing over the truth just a little. "Otherwise it was okay when we were forced to abandon it."

Aranya put her head in her hands. "I am *ruined*," she said. "The insurance companies will go broke trying to pay for the disaster, and our hurricane insurance will be worthless."

"Keep your chin up," Frank said. "I'm sure it'll be okay."

Callie gave the hotel owner a reassuring hug. "It'll all work out."

"Ask my lawyer about that," Beth Becker added.

The Bayport teens glared at her. Ms. Becker slumped back in the seat and closed her eyes.

"How did the fire start?" Joe asked Renee Aranya. "Was it lightning?"

"I don't know what happened," Aranya said. "I

had just finished a meeting with Jorge Tejeda, Rodrigo Lopez, and the mayor. We were picking a new date for the town meeting, as obviously today was not possible.

"The storm took the power and phone lines down, so we ended the meeting early. The others left, and I hurried to help with the hotel's emergency preparations. We already had many people in our basement shelter. Then the fire alarm went off."

"It's a good thing the alarm system was automatic," Frank said.

"*Sí,*" Aranya replied. "We tried to stop the fire, but . . ." She took a deep breath and couldn't continue for a moment. "It was useless. With the phone lines down, we could not contact the firemen. So we decided to evacuate the hotel. That is when you arrived."

Frank turned to Lucas McGill. "How did you happen to turn up at Casa Bonita?"

"A suspicious boy, aren't you?" The Gringo replied, smiling slightly. "Can't a man have lunch where he pleases?"

"You're saying it's just coincidence that you were there during the meeting with the town leaders?" Joe asked, incredulous.

"I wouldn't say it was *coincidence* . . . ," The Gringo said. "It was lucky for you and Ms. Becker that I was there, though."

Frank nodded. "I can't argue with that."

"I'm glad we got everyone out safely," Callie said.

"I wouldn't count those chickens yet," Joe replied. "Look."

Ahead of them lay the river that ran between Casa Bonita and the Hotel San Esteban. When the teenagers had arrived on the island, the river had been a placid watercourse that added to the island's beauty. Now, swollen by rain from the typhoon, it had grown into a raging monster. The river had flowed over its banks. They watched in horror as the last remnants of the bridge that had once spanned the river crumbled. In moments the only highway into San Esteban vanished.

"What about the bus?" Callie asked, panic in her voice.

"I see it," Frank said, pointing to the roadway on the other side. "It's moving down the highway through those trees. They made it."

"The bridge must have collapsed right after they crossed over," Joe said.

"But what about us?" Iola asked. Her eyes scanned the raging river and shattered bridge. "How will we get across?"

"Who's up for a swim?" Joe joked.

"I don't think we can stay with the van," Frank said. "If the storm gets any worse—and I think it will—we won't be safe here."

"The river narrows upstream," The Gringo said, "near the scenic falls. There's a footbridge above the falls that we could use. I can lead us there."

"Will the bridge still be safe?" Renee Aranya asked.

"We don't have any choice but to find out," Joe said. "You're sure you can lead us there safely?" he asked The Gringo.

The Gringo nodded. "I know this island like the back of my hand. I could find it blindfolded, even in this storm."

"Joe and I will help Ms. Becker," Frank said. "Callie, Iola, Ms. Aranya—follow Mr. McGill, and warn us about falling debris and other hazards."

"Check," Callie and Iola replied.

"Everybody ready?" Joe asked as he and Frank put Beth Becker's arms around their shoulders.

Everyone in the van nodded, and Iola opened the sliding door in the side of the vehicle. The wind buffeted them, trying to push them back in as they fought their way outside.

The Gringo led them up the river, keeping them a good distance back from the bank and well away from the torrent of floodwaters. As they wound their way up the hillside the riverbanks grew steeper and steeper.

"Not too far now," The Gringo said.

The rain quickly soaked them to the skin once

again, even under the Bayport teens' ponchos. Lightning flashed all around, and thunder shook the hills. The wind through the trees sounded like the hissing of a giant snake.

They quickly reached the pedestrian walkway across the river. It was a steel-cable suspension bridge—flimsy-looking, but clearly built to withstand harsh weather. The river below the span roared and surged, casting spray even up onto the walkway. The wind made the bridge sway terribly, but the seven of them safely made their way across. Beth Becker looked even paler by the time they got to the far side.

"Don't worry, lady," The Gringo said to her. "It's all downhill from here."

They hiked back into the forest, but soon veered off of the main path and onto a game trail.

"This way is shorter," The Gringo explained. "The hiking trail heads up into the hills before winding back toward town."

"Shorter is good," Frank said.

The Hardys and their companions hiked down the narrow path, Joe and Frank still helping Beth Becker whenever she needed it. Soon they were all muddy as well as wet, and most had taken an accidental slide or two.

Suddenly Joe stopped and listened. "Do you hear that?" he asked.

"It's just the wind," Callie replied.

"No," Joe said. "It's more than the wind. Something's coming."

They all turned and looked uphill. Behind them the trail seemed alive with writhing, wriggling bodies. Snakes covered the entire path.

13 Wildlife Rampage

The serpents surged downhill like a living river. Some were black, and others were green, red, or yellow. Behind the rainbow torrent of snakes came a stampede of other animals: deer, boars, monkeys, and lizards.

"They're running from the storm!" Frank shouted. "Get off the path!"

He and Joe dragged Beth Becker off the trail, while the others scurried into the brush. They scrambled up into the trees, but the slippery bark made climbing almost impossible. Despite this, all of them managed to get their feet far enough off the ground that a snake could slither harmlessly under them.

The thundering stampede of frightened animals

passed by quickly. Soon even the slowest lizards had disappeared around the bend in the trail below.

"That's the trouble with game trails," Joe said. "You never know when game animals might want to use them." He wiped the rain and sweat from his brow as they all lowered themselves to the ground.

"I know a way through the jungle from here," The Gringo said. "It's shorter, but harder to navigate."

"I vote for staying off the game trails," Callie said, raising her hand. Iola, Aranya, and Ms. Becker raised their hands too.

The brothers nodded. "Looks like it's decided," Frank said. "Let's go."

"Don't worry," The Gringo added. "It's not too far now."

The next time the trail turned, they went straight. The wind and the rain still lashed at them mercilessly, and they took frequent stops to gather their strength. When the wind pushed the trees aside, they glimpsed Nuevo Esteban's church tower. It wasn't very far off, and this gave them all hope. Soon they reached the outskirts of the small city.

As the tired teens and their companions staggered into town they noticed that the streets were deserted. Water covered the roads.

"The main storm shelter is in the high school," Renee Aranya said. "It's on this side of town—it's not too far away."

"That's good," Callie replied. "I don't know how much farther I can walk. My feet feel like solid blisters inside my sneakers."

"I'm looking forward to getting something in my stomach," Joe said.

They quickly reached the crowded emergency shelter. The high school was one of the newest buildings in town and had been built in accordance with all the modern safety guidelines. The gym, which served as the shelter, had concrete walls and a reinforced roof. The solid construction reduced the howl of the wind to a dull noise and made the nightmare of the storm seem a little less scary.

The gym was crowded, especially since the trouble at Casa Bonita had left so many vacationers without a shelter to stay in. Still, the big, open space was dry and warm, and a welcome relief for the tired teenagers. Emergency lights lit the dark interior, and volunteer workers were handing out blankets and hot soup, or tending to the injured.

Renee Aranya had a joyful reunion with her staff, and even Beth Becker seemed happy to be there. The Gringo quickly slipped into the crowd and disappeared. The Hardys and their girlfriends found a quiet corner in which they could sit and relax. They huddled close to one another under two blankets and sipped soup. They saw people they knew in the crowd. Jorge Tejeda and the mayor moved through the room, quietly consoling people.

Rodrigo Lopez, from the Hotel San Esteban, did the same.

"I wonder if he's running for office too," Joe commented.

They also spotted Luis, the handyman from the town hall, and Jose and Pablo Ruiz from the rental agency. Both brothers looked worried, as did most of the people in the room. A collective, concerned whisper filled the air.

"I bet Jose is wishing he'd stayed on Kendall Key," Frank said.

"I'm almost wishing *I* had stayed in Bayport," Callie replied. "I really need to get in touch with my folks. I'm sure they're freaking out about the storm. There must be a working phone somewhere in here—or some way to get a message out." She stood and looked around for a phone to use.

"Good idea," Frank said. "When you talk to your folks, have them tell our parents that we're okay too. There's no sense in all of us tying up the available lines."

Iola stood up as well.

"What's wrong?" Joe asked. "Callie can talk to your folks too."

"I need to find Angela," she said. "I don't see her around."

"Maybe she's at another shelter," Joe suggested.

"This shelter is probably in touch with the others," Iola said. "I'm going to check."

"Okay," Joe said. "Would you bring some coffee when you come back?"

"Sure will," Iola replied. She smiled at Joe, and she and Callie wandered off on their errands.

The brothers leaned back against the wall. "Not the kind of vacation the girls had hoped for," Frank finally said.

"We'll make it up to them somehow," Joe replied.

"The storm's not to blame for all our troubles, though," Frank said. "Storms don't slash tires or shoot blowguns."

"And it wasn't even cloudy when someone set El Diablo free," Joe said, continuing his brother's thought. He shook his head. "Someone is stirring things up on this island. The question is who, and why?"

"It was very convenient for Lucas McGill to be at Casa Bonita when it caught fire," Frank said.

"He was there at the boat hijacking and when the bull got loose too," Joe said. "And he was at the town hall, come to think of it."

"He's a shady character, just like Angela said," Frank observed. "No doubt about it. But what could he gain from all this chaos?"

"What would anyone gain?" Joe replied.

"It could be some kind of hotel insurance scam," Frank said. "Ms. Aranya could have torched her place for insurance and set up the other stuff to make it look like a general pattern of crime."

"Or Lopez could be looking to get rid of his hotel's competition," Joe suggested.

"Either way, it seems a bit extreme," Frank said. "This kind of trouble could hurt the whole island's economy."

As the brothers pondered the mysterious case they found themselves thrust into, they felt the tension in the room grow. A crowd gathered in the center of the gymnasium, and the mayor stepped on top of a chair in the middle of the throng.

"Everyone stay calm!" the mayor said. "This building is safe. We have plenty of food and fresh water. Everyone will be all right."

"What about our homes?" someone called.

"And our businesses?" asked another.

"Tourism is already down," said a third. "We will be ruined!"

"All this trouble has made our property nearly worthless!"

"Never mind all that," someone said. "I have family missing out in the storm. What am I going to do about that?"

The murmur grew to a dull roar. The mayor waved her hands, palms down, to quiet the crowd. Rodrigo Lopez stepped forward and stood on a chair next to the mayor. "I am organizing volunteer search parties to assist the police," he said. "We will look for missing people and help anyone who is injured. We won't wait for the storm to end. If you are interested, meet me by the main doors." He got down and headed in that direction, followed by a handful of people.

Jorge Tejeda stepped up onto the empty chair. "I have faith in our town," he said. "Nuevo Esteban will bounce back from this disaster. I will help locate buyers for those who cannot afford to rebuild damaged property themselves and for those who do not wish to rebuild—as I have done after past storms. Recovery will be a long, arduous task, but Nuevo Esteban will rise again. This I promise you."

The two short speeches calmed the crowd. Most of those present drifted back to their personal business. Shortly thereafter Iola and Callie returned. They looked worried.

"What's wrong?" Frank asked Callie.

"Did you talk to your parents?" Joe added.

"I got them on the phone," Callie replied. "But we couldn't find Angela."

"She's not at the other shelters, and no one seems to have seen her," Iola said.

The brothers stood up. "We'll go with the search parties," Frank said, "and try to find her."

"You two stay here," Joe added. "No sense in all of us trudging into the storm again."

"Besides, we need someone here in case Angela shows up," Frank finished.

Iola and Callie glanced nervously at each other.

Callie finally said, "Okay. Keep the heroics to a minimum, though. All right?"

Frank nodded at her and gave her a quick hug. "You bet."

"Don't get hurt," Iola said to Joe.

The younger Hardy smiled. "What, me? Never."

The brothers joined the small crowd gathered with Lopez near the doorway. They saw Luis the handyman, Jose Ruiz, Pablo Ruiz, and Jorge Tejeda among the crowd as well.

"I guess Tejeda had to volunteer," Joe whispered.

"Only if he wants to be reelected," Frank whispered back.

Lopez and his volunteers handed out flares, flashlights, compact emergency blankets, and plastic ponchos for those who needed them. Some volunteers requested to check a specific area, while others offered to go on general patrols. Joe and Frank asked to be assigned to Angela's neighborhood. One of Lopez's people gave them a map with an area marked off in waterproof marker.

"Be careful," the volunteer said. "If you find something you can't handle, light a flare and come back here. We'll contact the police to help out. Whatever you do, stay away from the shoreline. Those waves will carry you out to sea, and no one will ever find your bodies."

The brothers indicated that they understood, took a moment to orient themselves, and then headed out into the storm once more. They saw a few small groups leaving at the same time, but the driving rain soon hid their fellow searchers.

Angela's neighborhood wasn't far from the high school, but getting there through Nuevo Esteban's winding streets in the tough weather proved tricky. The Hardys were forced several times to change their route because of flooding or a downed power-line.

As darkness closed in around them the brothers reached the small residential street where Iola's cousin lived. Angela's apartment was on the second floor of a traditional adobe building. A wooden staircase on the side of the building led to her door.

Through the rain the Hardys saw that Angela's stairway had collapsed. The door to her apartment opened onto nothing but the rain-saturated air. Frank took out their own flashlight, and Joe took out the new one they'd gotten at the shelter. They ran to the base of the stairs and searched in the rubble, all the while calling Angela's name.

"Here I am!" they heard a voice reply from above.

They looked up and saw Angela silhouetted in the doorway of her apartment. "The stairs collapsed just as I was about to leave," she said. "I couldn't get down safely, and the phones are out, so I stayed inside."

"Smart," Frank called up to her.

"We'll help you down and bring you to the shelter," Joe added.

Angela went to grab her raincoat and a bag full of belongings of sentimental value. The brothers moved cautiously over the ruins of the stairway. The rain made everything slippery, and the wind made balancing difficult. Working carefully, they finally lowered Angela to the ground.

"Let's get back to the high school," Frank said, starting back the way they'd come.

"Wait," Angela called above the wind. "I know a shortcut."

The brothers followed Iola's cousin as fast as they could through the back streets of Nuevo Esteban. As they crossed behind an old factory, though, something flashed in front of their faces and stuck in a nearby door.

"A blowgun dart!" Joe said.

As they realized what it was a shot rang out in the twilight.

"And a sniper, too!" Frank said.

Angela's eyes went wide. "We're trapped!"

14 Caught in the Crossfire

"Get down!" Joe said.

The three teens crouched and pressed themselves against the factory wall opposite where the dart had hit.

"Do you see anyone?" Frank asked.

Joe shook his head. Another shot rang out. "We need to find better cover," he said. "Let's go!" With that, the younger Hardy took off, back the way they'd come. Frank and Angela followed closely behind.

A dart whizzed by them as they ran, barely missing Frank's shoulder. The gun fired again, but with the noise of the wind and the rain, they couldn't locate where the sound came from.

"There's a cave-tour entrance up ahead," Angela said as they ran. "It leads to the old bootlegger tunnels."

"Good idea," Frank replied. "They can't catch us in a crossfire underground—I hope."

They ducked into an alley, then climbed over a fence. Another shot sounded as they landed on the other side. They didn't even attempt to look for the sniper; they just kept running as fast as they could.

"Here it is," Angela announced after running a ways. She indicated a boarded-up ticket stand with TOURS OF THE UNDERGROUND painted above the sales window. In the middle of the wall next to the stand was a padlocked door.

"Pretty ratty-looking tour outfit for a politician," Frank commented.

"Tejeda is notoriously cheap," Angela replied, glancing around nervously. "Most of his properties are run down. But he is kind to the poor and fights for government aid."

"Cheap or not, this lock looks tough," Joe said, examining the entrance.

Frank reeled back and gave the old wooden door his best martial arts kick. The wood around the latch splintered, and the lock fell off. "Good thing the door wasn't," he replied with a smirk.

"You know," Joe said as they fled into the darkness

of the underground, "I'd feel a little better about this if I had some idea of who could be shooting at us."

"Yeah, and why," Frank agreed.

They headed deeper into the old tunnels, trying to put as much distance between themselves and the snipers as they could. The passages they moved through were similar to the ones the Hardys and their girlfriends had been trapped in near the shore; these were old lava tunnels, worn smooth by time and water.

"Do you know where these tunnels go?" Frank asked Angela.

"Not really," she said. "I've only been in them once or twice. And no one knows all of them. The caverns form an underground honeycomb on this end of the island. Some go to hidden places on the coast. Others head into the mountains."

"We found one of those coastline tunnels yesterday," Joe said. "The boat stolen from the Casa Bonita beach was stashed inside. Could there be a connection between here and there?"

Angela shrugged. "Maybe. This place used to be a bootlegger's paradise. I've never heard of a tour going out to the coast from here, though."

A shot echoed down the tunnel. The three teens froze, but none of them saw the gun flash or the person firing. "Keep moving," Frank whispered.

"And keep quiet. They may be firing blind, hoping to scare us."

"It's working," Angela whispered nervously.

They moved cautiously down the passage until they came to a boarded-up side tunnel. "I think we can squeeze past these boards," Joe whispered. "Do you have any idea of what's inside?"

Angela shook her head. "They've blocked off tunnels where the tour doesn't go."

Joe used his flashlight to see through the cracks. "There's a passage, but I can't see what's at the end of it."

"Let's go," Frank whispered.

The brothers carefully pulled away one of the boards blocking the tunnel's entrance. All three of them crawled inside. They crept down the passage until it came to a bend, then they stopped and caught their breath.

"Who would want to do this?" Joe asked, frustrated by the whole situation. "Jamie Escobar might want to get back at us for showing him up, but who else has a motive?"

"Maybe our troubles are just part of a larger crime scheme," Frank replied. "I suspect that the Beth Becker hijacking, the collapse of the town hall, these sniper attacks, and even the fires at our hotel and bungalows are all related. So much trouble in so little time. It's unlikely to be coincidence."

"Casa Bonita caught fire?" Angela asked. "Is everyone all right?"

"Yeah, everyone got out fine—thanks in part to The Gringo, who always seems to be around when trouble happens," Joe said.

"I warned you about him," said Iola's cousin. "But how would he profit from all of this? How would anyone? This is hurting the tourism we all need to live."

"Lopez might benefit from hurting Casa Bonita," Frank said. "Or maybe one of the local politicians is hoping to turn this into a clean-up-our-streets campaign."

Joe frowned. "That seems like a twisted way to get reelected."

"People have gone further than this," Frank replied.

"So, we've got Escobar, Lopez, The Gringo, the mayor, and Tejeda on our list of suspects," Joe said. "We could include Aranya, too."

Frank shook his head and sighed in exasperation. "There could be dozens of people in Nuevo Esteban with motives we don't know about."

"Yeah," Joe replied. "Too many suspects—but not enough with really obvious motives."

"Let's go over what we know one more time," Frank said.

"Hold it!" Joe said. "I hear someone. Let's move farther down the tunnel."

The three teens did as Joe suggested. They turned around two more bends before finally coming to a small chamber. The room had nearly rectangular walls; it must have been created by bootleggers at some time in the past. A large box leaned against one wall. Leading from it was a long wire, which stretched out an exit on the opposite side of the room.

The Hardys and Angela froze. The box was clearly marked TNT.

"Why would someone store explosives down here?" Angela asked.

"The better question," Frank said, "is why is it wired to explode—and who's on the other end with the detonator?" He and Joe knelt by the box and quickly disconnected the leads.

"Whoever it is will be disappointed when this particular candle doesn't light," Joe said. "This is way too far to go for an insurance scam."

"Unless," Frank said, "you're insuring the whole town." He shone his flashlight down the exit tunnel into the darkness. The wire they'd disconnected trailed into another chamber a short distance away. "Come on," he said. "I want to see what's at the other end of this wire."

Angela looked around nervously. "Maybe we should wait here," she said.

"Wait until whoever wants to blow this place up

notices we've messed with his handiwork?" Joe asked.

Angela shook her head, and the three of them moved into the next chamber. There they found a similar setup. Once again Frank and Joe disconnected the wire.

"I'm thinking," Frank said, "that bombing enough tunnels could seriously endanger large portions of the town."

"And if you did it during a storm," Joe added, following his brother's train of thought, "you might be able to blame it on the typhoon."

Frank nodded.

"I hear someone!" Angela said. The brothers turned off their flashlights and pressed up against the walls on either side of the tunnel. Angela did the same.

A moment later a light came flitting down the tunnel, playing against the rock walls as if it was searching for something—or someone.

The Hardys and Angela held their breath.

Slowly a figure entered the room. He held a flashlight in one hand and a gun in the other. Before he could spot them, Frank and Joe pounced.

The man tried to grab the brothers, but Joe tackled him low and Frank grabbed him high. The elder Hardy knocked the gun out of the sniper's grip, while Joe pulled the would-be assassin down. The man's pistol and his flashlight skidded across the chamber.

A quick one-two combination by the brothers sent the sniper to the floor, unconscious.

Angela retrieved the flashlight. Frank moved the gun far away while Joe shone the light on their pursuer.

"Jamie Escobar," Joe said. "I can't say I'm surprised."

"I am," Frank replied. "This case seems too complex for one tough guy out for revenge."

They tied Escobar with his own belt, gagged him with a strip of cloth Frank ripped from his shirt, and dragged him to the side of the chamber far from the gun. Angela patted him down, making sure he didn't have any concealed weapons. The only thing she found was some identification in his pocket.

Angela's eyes went wide. "Look at what I found in his wallet!"

She held up the wallet she'd retrieved from his pocket, and tossed it to Joe. Inside was a San Esteban government ID and badge.

"He's an Internal Security agent?" Joe asked, surprised.

"That doesn't make any sense," Frank said. "If he were government security, why would he be shooting at us?"

"And what about the explosives?" Joe said. "What was Escobar up to with that?" He looked at the bound man.

"He wasn't up to anything," said a voice from behind them. "In fact, I'm sure Señor Escobar wanted to prevent us from setting off the dynamite. Now, bring that gun over here, or I will have to harm you."

15 The Big Blowup

Jose Ruiz stepped from the shadows. In his hand he held a revolver pointed at the brothers. "My boss will be very pleased that you have eliminated the troublemaker Escobar," he said. Jose grinned, showing his missing tooth. "I hope you will not mind if the boss does not thank you in person; he is a very busy man."

"Is the rental business slow, Jose?" Frank asked. He slowly went to pick up the gun and handed it over as instructed.

Jose shrugged as he carefully reached for the weapon. "It is good enough for my brother, perhaps—but not good enough for me."

"So *you* sabotaged the plane we rented from

137

you," Joe said. "Why? To hurt your brother, or to harm the tourist business on San Esteban?"

Jose's dark eyes narrowed. "You are far too smart for your own good, *Americano*," he said. "Now that I have had a moment to consider, I think I *will* hurt you."

Angela Martinez screamed. The cavern magnified the sound, making it almost deafening. The earsplitting noise caused Jose to flinch as he pulled the trigger.

Joe flung himself across the floor in a barrel roll, and Frank ducked to one side. The shot went between the brothers, and before Jose could fire again, they were on top of him. Joe knocked Jose's legs out from under him, while Frank clouted the man on the jaw. Jose went down like a sack of flour. Joe hit him one final time, just to make sure he didn't get up.

"Good work!" Frank said to Angela.

"I-I was just frightened," she said, her voice shaking.

"Good work anyway," Joe said, smiling.

It took the brothers only a minute to tie Jose with his own coat. As they trussed up their prisoner Jamie Escobar groaned.

"He's coming to, I think," Angela said.

Escobar's eyes flickered open, but he still looked dazed. Angela ungagged him. "What happened?" he asked.

"We thought you were shooting at us," Joe replied warily.

"I . . . was not shooting at you," Escobar said. "I was shooting at the man who was shooting at you with the blowgun."

"Was that Jose?" Frank asked.

Escobar shook his head wearily. "No," he said. "It was . . ." His eyes rolled back and he lapsed into unconsciousness once more.

"If Jose is here," Angela said, "then his brother, Pablo, must be the man behind the trouble."

"I don't think so," Frank said. "Remember what Jose said about the rental business being enough for his brother, but not him?"

Joe nodded. "Besides, how would a rental business profit from hurting the tourist trade on San Esteban?"

"How would *anyone*?" Angela asked.

"I'm betting that whoever is at the other end of this wire can answer that question," Frank said, looking at the line they'd disconnected from the TNT charges.

"And I think we have a pretty good idea who that person is," Joe added.

"Take care of Agent Escobar," Frank said to Angela. "And Joe and I will take care of whoever's on the other end of this line."

Angela nodded, and the brothers went off into the tunnel, following the detonator wire.

The passages twisted and turned as they snaked under the city. The brothers saw many more packages of TNT on their way, but they knew they didn't have time to stop and disconnect them all—not if they hoped to stop the villain behind the plot.

They ran as quickly as they could, knowing that at any moment the mastermind of this awful scheme could set off the dynamite. "Let's hope," Frank said as they sprinted down the passages, "that he's waiting for Jose to return before pushing that plunger."

Tracing the wire, they soon came to a ladder leading up to a trapdoor. They heard voices through the open hatchway above. "What is taking Jose so long down there, do you think?" one asked.

"Some trouble with the connections, perhaps," replied another voice.

"You don't think," said the first voice, "that he ran into those meddlesome teenagers or that spy in the tunnels, do you? They were near the tour entrance when I lost them."

There was a pause before the other, more resonant voice replied, "I doubt it. No one knows those passages but us. Just in case, though, we'll detonate the TNT in five minutes—whether Jose returns or not."

The two voices laughed.

The Hardys approached the bottom of the ladder and listened carefully. They heard possibly two or three people moving around upstairs. The brothers waited until the sounds moved away from the trapdoor before climbing up the ladder.

Poking their heads out cautiously, they saw the dark interior of a deteriorating factory. Rain dripped through the ceiling, and they could hear the typhoon winds howling outside. Standing near the ladder, with his back to the boys, was a man dressed in overalls. He was rummaging in an old tool chest. A well-dressed man fiddled with what looked like a detonator box on the opposite side of the room. "Give me some pliers, would you, Luis?" he asked.

Luis turned to answer, and when he did, he spotted the Hardys. Before he could say anything, the brothers jumped through the trapdoor and rushed toward the criminals. Joe took the handyman, while Frank ran over to the deep-voiced stranger.

The handyman pulled a dart out of his coveralls and popped it into his blowgun. Before he could shoot, though, Joe tackled him to the ground. Luis struggled, but he was no match for the athletic teenager. Joe shouldered the handyman's pudgy gut, then finished him off with a solid uppercut.

The well-dressed man turned as the elder Hardy closed in on him.

"Jorge Tejeda," Frank said. "I thought so."

"Pretty smart, *turista*," the politician replied.

Frank aimed a chop at Tejeda's collarbone. The older man ducked out of the way, dropped to the floor, and swept Frank's legs out from under him with a spin kick.

Tejeda laughed and bounced to his feet. "Before I was a politician," he said, "I was the island's *capoeira* champion."

Before Frank could recover, Tejeda dropped him with a vicious kick to the jaw. The evil politician reached for the detonator box. As he did he shot Joe a glance that said, *Too late*. Joe grabbed the blowgun, put it to his lips, and fired.

His aim wasn't perfect, but the shot scratched across the back of Tejeda's hand. The politician drew back in surprise, giving Frank just enough time to recover. Ignoring the spots dancing before his eyes, Frank spun across the floor, imitating the kick Tejeda had used to bring him to the ground.

His blow caught the politician behind the knees, and Tejeda toppled like a stout tree. Joe sprinted in, and working together, the Hardys quickly subdued their foe.

"Did he say he was a master of Copacabana?" Joe asked as they tied Tejeda and Luis up.

"*Capoeira*," Frank said as he pulled the knot tight around the politician's wrists. "It's a Brazilian martial art."

"Oh, good," Joe replied. "For a moment I thought he was going to try to sing us to death."

The worst of the storm was over by the time the Hardys set out their flares to attract the police. The city authorities were shocked to discover their most prominent politician had been behind such a dastardly plot. Fortunately Jamie Escobar—who easily recovered from his earlier tussle with the brothers—arrived in time to back up the Hardys' story.

All of them spent the night in the Nuevo Esteban police station, and the brothers rejoined their girlfriends the following morning. By that time Hurricane Hilary had moved back out to sea.

In gratitude for their services the island tourism bureau gave the teens rooms at the Hotel San Esteban for the final days of their vacation.

"What a nightmare!" Iola said after they'd recovered their things from the stranded Jeep and moved into their new rooms.

The four of them and Angela Martinez sat in the living room of the girls' suite, looking out over the bay. The waters of the harbor were still gray and gloomy, but sunshine had begun to peek through the receding storm clouds.

"I'll say," Callie agreed. "I'm glad this hotel has an indoor pool. The beach is a wreck!"

"And probably will be for months," Angela added.

"I hope that Ms. Aranya has enough insurance to rebuild her hotel and bungalows," Callie said.

"She should be okay," Frank replied.

"What she doesn't get from her insurance, she should be able to recover from Tejeda's holding companies," Joe added. "The value of his business and real estate properties should cover the damage he and his sidekicks did."

"And he won't be needing money where he's going," Iola said with a satisfied smile.

Callie sighed. "So our vacation was ruined by a greedy politician."

"And a typhoon," Iola added.

Joe smiled. "Not even Tejeda could arrange that—though he and his cohorts *did* try to use the storm to further their scheme."

"Exactly which one of them tried to shoot us?" Callie asked.

"Luis, the handyman," Joe replied.

"The first time Luis used the blowgun," Frank said, "he just wanted to scare tourists off the island."

"That's the same reason they set the fires, both to our bungalows and to Casa Bonita, and slashed the tires of our Jeep," Joe continued. "The previous muggings, the theft of Beth Becker's rental boat, the creatures in the rooms, and the release of El Diablo were all part of the same plan."

"Either Jose, Luis, or Tejeda was always nearby when the 'accidents' happened," Frank said. "Because they were working together, it was nearly impossible to figure out who was doing all of these things, and why. Luis's job also came in handy, as it diverted suspicion of their sabotage of the town hall—and probably other incidents as well."

"The perfect man for the cover-up," Callie remarked.

"We weren't the only tourists targeted, though sometimes it seemed that way," Joe said. "Most of the problems went unreported. Tourism and hotel officials didn't want island business to be hurt, so they covered some incidents up."

Frank nodded. "The second time Luis used the blowgun, he was trying to scare us away from the deserted factory where he, Jose, and Tejeda were setting up the detonator. We never would have found that if Angela hadn't taken us on a shortcut back to the storm shelter."

"I'll never take that shortcut again!" Angela said.

"Agent Escobar was watching the factory and fired at Luis to try to protect us," Joe explained. "The government suspected Tejeda was up to something, but they didn't know what. When Luis came after us, Escobar chased and shot at him— which explains all the gunshots. Luis returned after Escobar followed Angela, Frank, and me into the old bootlegger tunnels. Escobar was the one Frank and I chased that day in the rain. At that point, because of the El Diablo incident, he thought we might be in on Tejeda's scheme."

"Luis's shooting at you convinced him otherwise," Angela added.

Callie rubbed her head. "This was a pretty complex scheme to wreck the island's tourism."

"Tejeda wasn't really aiming to ruin tourism," Frank replied. "His true goal was to drive down real estate prices, while solidifying his political position as 'friend of the poor.'"

"It was a good plan," Joe said. "They cause crime in Nuevo Esteban and then take credit for cleaning it up. By the time tourism rebounded, Tejeda would have owned the best properties on this side of the island—and he would have bought them for a song."

"Just like he bought the underground tour business and those other properties over the years," Angela said.

"Owning the bootlegger tour business gave him access to the tunnels he and his gang needed to pull off their crimes," Frank said. "They could move between the city and the coast with no one seeing them. It also gave them a place to stash money and stolen goods, like the speedboat. When the storm blew in, Tejeda saw an opportunity to put their 'urban renewal' plan into high gear. They could dynamite the tunnels under key areas and then blame the storm for the collapse of the old tunnels and the damage to the city."

"Then they could swoop in and pick up the pieces," Iola said.

"The disaster would have killed the real estate

market in a way that would have taken months, or maybe years, to accomplish otherwise," Joe said. "Then Tejeda could step in—both financially and politically—and be the town's savior."

"Having Luis in the town repair office, and Jose in the tourist rental business, made the sabotage that much easier," Frank said.

"Then, it was Jose and the handyman who hijacked Beth Becker's speedboat," Callie said.

Frank and Joe nodded. "And Jose who sabotaged our plane," Frank added.

"Working against his own brother!" Angela said, shocked.

"Pablo Ruiz wasn't involved at all," Joe said. "He was just a patsy."

"Okay, I get all that," Iola said. "And I understand why Escobar was constantly showing up—he was an agent working the case. But what about Lucas McGill?"

"We think The Gringo was probably trying to find out who was behind the scheme—either to stop the trouble or, more likely, to get a cut," Joe said. "That's why he kept popping up like a bad penny. But who knows for sure."

"That's The Gringo's luck," Angela said. "Other people get caught, and he gets away scot-free." She threw up her hands in exasperation.

"Oh, I'm sure that he'll slip up one day," Joe said.

"Someone will catch him," Frank replied.

"Well, I hope it's not you two who put him behind bars," Iola said, winking playfully at Joe.

Callie looked at Frank. "Or if it is," she added, "I hope it's not during our next vacation!"

Test your detective skills with these spine-tingling Aladdin Mysteries!

The Star-Spangled Secret
By K. M. Kimball

Mystery at Kittiwake Bay
By Joyce Stengel

Scared Stiff
By Willo Davis Roberts

O'Dwyer & Grady
Starring in Acting Innocent
By Eileen Heyes

Ghosts in the Gallery
By Barbara Brooks Wallace

The York Trilogy By Phyllis Reynolds Naylor

Shadows on the Wall

Faces in the Water

Footprints at the Window

Don't miss these other great baseball titles from Aladdin Paperbacks!

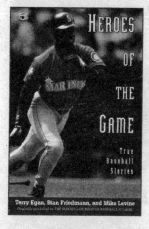

*Heroes of the Game:
True Baseball Stories*
by Terry Egan, Stan Friedman, and Mike Levine
(0-689-81352-X $4.50 US, $5.99 CAN)
True stories about the successes and trials of major stars, average players, and even baseball fans.

How to Snag Major League Baseballs: More Than 100 Tested Tricks That Really Work
by Zack Hample
(0-689-82331-2 $3.99 US, $5.50 CAN)
Learn how to bring home the ultimate souvenir from a game by someone who ought to know—he's snagged over 1,000 major league balls!

Aladdin Paperbacks
Simon & Schuster Children's Publishing
www.SimonSaysKids.com

Wacky things keep happening in
Middleburg—join in the fun with the

BERNIE MAGRUDER MYSTERIES

BY PHYLLIS REYNOLDS NAYLOR